The

Sara Alexi is the a   the Greek Village Series.
She divides her time between England and a small village
in Greece.

http://facebook.com/authorsaraalexi

Sara Alexi

THE RELUCTANT BAKER

oneiro

Published by Oneiro Press 2015

This edition 2015

ISBN-13: 978-1511497879
ISBN-10: 1511497874

Also by Sara Alexi

The Illegal Gardener
Black Butterflies
The Explosive Nature of Friendship
The Gypsy's Dream
The Art of Becoming Homeless
In the Shade of the Monkey Puzzle Tree
A Handful of Pebbles
The Unquiet Mind
Watching the Wind Blow

The moss under her fingers is too wet for a sure grip. Crouched as she is, her heels raised on the tufts of grass by the dry stone wall, Ellie is tipping forward. Shifting to lean her shoulders against the stones, her fingers let go and she tucks her icy hands in between her legs and her stomach, down in her crotch, seeking warmth that is not there. The incessant rain plasters her hair to her head. It drips down her collar, a stream running the length of her spine. The wind is less on this side of the wall but it still bites deep. The cars on the main road on the other side of the wall hiss with the spray thrown up by their wheels as they pass.

She shivers.

How long would it take for hypothermia to set in?

Her teeth chatter and she dips her head as low as she can.

First, she will shiver as her body's warmth is sucked inside to keep her organs functioning. She is at that stage already. Then her limbs will become numb as the blood ceases to flow to the extremities. Already she cannot feel her toes. There is a searing pain through her fingers. It fits. It all fits. It has been just one blindingly sharp tear at her life after another. How naïve of her to try to think she could make anything better by going to Greece.

As hypothermia takes its grip there is a point, she has read, when she will no longer feel cold.

3

Apparently you feel pleasantly warm by that stage; your mind plays tricks, becomes confused. Then gradually, her breathing will slow, the beat of her heart will grow faint and maybe, just maybe, someone will find her in a week or two's time. But that will be after the foxes and the smaller creatures in the grass have found her first and her return to the earth will have begun.

Chapter One

Chapter 1

His mind is awake before his body is. His mouth hangs open, relaxed, free-flowing dreams still there, almost tangible. His mind floats from one bizarre image to the next. It is exquisite to be caught like this, between waking and sleeping. Fragile pictures, illusions, delusions, nonsense. Sunlight, hills, a boat floating on olive trees, loaves of bread in amongst the goats, Natasha holding a crook. Swimming in silver, further and further out into a darkened nightclub with angelic music and flashing lights. Flying in blue, made of nothing but light. The precious feeling of how unimpeded his mind is, with no tightness, no worries, no memories, just mirages flowing.

He wakes automatically these days, savouring these moments, hanging onto the creativity before his mind begins to take control, the tedium of everyday thoughts returning. He has no will to open his eyes. The room is black, its sparseness invisible, the plain wooden chest of drawers and chair only shadows, the unadorned white walls reflecting what little light there is, dawn not yet breaking outside the window.

A sharp tap comes through the wall from the bedroom next door. Tuc, tic. The first tap tightens his shoulder muscles, the second those in his neck and third those in his jaw and he grinds his teeth.

Eyes still shut, Loukas sits, rests a minute still floating in and out of the impressions in his mind; delicate touches, light feathery kisses, flowers with transparent petals, the sensation of weightlessness. Then he stands, the bare wooden floorboards creaking their objection, reality pressing him awake. Anticipation fills him as he pulls open the window so he can push the shutters outwards—there may be a breath of cool air. He would sleep with the windows open all night if it wasn't for the mosquitoes. His actions are automatic, guided by habit as he is still without full consciousness. There is no breeze, no cool air today. A dim glow comes from the sole streetlight that is mounted on the wall by the *kafeneio*. Where its illumination cannot reach, it creates long fingers of ink that creep behind the kiosk, up the side of the palm tree, and around the small, empty fountain. Loukas' room above the bakery overlooks the square where the fountain and the palm tree jostle for space with the kiosk, which sells cigarettes and other small items.

The whitewashed village houses loom like ghosts from the shadows, offering up no pinpricks of light from cracks in closed shutters. Even the farmers who hunt in the early dawn are still dreaming of hilltops full of rabbits. Their dogs, too, are asleep. It will be an hour yet before the dawn telegraph of

7

barks and howls and cockerels crowing. There is nothing to indicate that the village is alive, that hundreds of people live here, that the day will bring bustle and gossip. For now, they are all safe behind closed blue shutters in the relative cool of the night.

Loukas clenches his fists and raises them to his ears, elbows upwards, before punching the air above his head, the energy of youth coursing through his veins. His face twists, mouth opens wide, his eyes shut tight as he sucks in oxygen. It helps him to surface. With blurry eyes, he reluctantly reaches for his trousers, which are slung over the back of the chair, and his t-shirt, which lies crumpled on the floor. It is nicer to be naked and cool. Now that would cause a stir!

Sitting on the wooden chair to lace his boots, out of the corner of his eye, he catches the pictures by his bed. One of his sister, the other Natasha, still there, smiling at him. She will always be there smiling, unchanging, her eyes watching him as he moves around the room. It's nearly a year now. The loss has settled as a constant hollow in his chest that weighs down his breathing. A weight that is changing, no longer so much for her as for himself, his endless life ahead of him in which he is on his own. Grief that has almost turned into self-pity. The very person who was meant to set him free has, by her death, trapped him.

The rapping on the adjoining wall repeats itself. His feet on the landing and down the uncarpeted wooden stairs are loud enough to let them know he is up. This is not what he ever envisaged for his life, but then, he did not envisage his early marriage or her early death, either. Stomping down the stairs, he makes no effort to quieten his footsteps. He's up, why should they not be?

A few more minutes of semi-sleep are part of his ritual as he waits for the water to heat over the stove. With two spoonfuls of sugar, the water glistens. A quick stir and it is dissolved enough for the coffee to be added. The grounds sit on the bubbling sweet water, the rich brown turning darker around the edges as it absorbs the solution, its own heaviness sucking it under. Loukas' eyes close, his head drops forward and he jolts awake. The coffee will boil over if he doesn't watch it now and he will have to start again. How many times has he done that?

The frothing mass on top of the coffee rises slowly at first and then suddenly dashes for the rim. Lifting it off just in time, he pours it into his waiting cup and takes it from the kitchen through to the *fournos*, the bakery that connects the house and shop.

The stone-flagged floor is swept and pale from years of scrubbing, the central wooden table worn smooth with kneaded dough. Wooden raising troughs are stacked against the stone oven door, uniform and blanched with use. Sacks of flour stand, sagging around their middles. Their top corners, twisted like ears, droop as if they too are snoozing.

The dough machine gleams as usual in its corner, scrubbed clean and ready for use. It is a fine contraption, welded together by the local mechanic out of parts scavenged from his workshop, the result of ingenuity and deliberation, and many breaks for coffee, at a fraction of the cost of a commercial model.

Natasha was so proud of him when he finally brought it home. If he had to do it again today, he would build it bigger, have it knead ten kilos of bread at a time, twenty even. But back then, the thought of a machine mixing just three kilos was enough to spur them all on. Every five minutes, another three kilos mixed and ready to rise. It was a lot quicker than working by hand and afforded extra hours in bed, Natasha wrapping her arms around him, not allowing him to rise until he had made good use of the extra time.

Balancing his coffee cup on an upended dough trough, Loukas goes out to the back of the building, into the dark, and returns with a sack of olive logs, sawn and split to the right size. Once the fire under the still-warm oven is stoked, he opens the small window at the side of the building and pulls up a painted wooden chair to catch some of the dawn's cool air, to accompany his caffeine fix. There is nothing to see through the window, which opens on the alley at the back of the building, the stone wall opposite an arm's reach away. But it will be the only time he is not sweating, until the same time tomorrow.

First, it will be the work that brings beads of perspiration to his forehead, the heaving and lifting of the sacks, weighing the ingredients, shaping the mixed dough and giving it the final hand knead before he cuts it and lays each flattened sphere on a muslin cloth to put in the wooden dough troughs to rise. When all that is done, the raw heat of the oven will ensure his sweating continues as he paddles loaves in and out, swapping them around inside the oven's cavernous mouth so each has its turn to cook and brown in the prime spots. And when this is done, the sun will be at its highest in the sky.

He will have a brief sleep mid-afternoon when the shade offers no cool, and when he wakes, there will be a little time to himself to read, walk, or make orders for the bakery and then he will be in bed again before the slight drop in temperature that the evening brings at this time of year. At the height of summer, neither the evening nor the dawn will bring such relief.

But right now, a whisper of wind plays with the fine longer hairs above his forehead. Round his neck, his hair is shorn in an attempt to stay cool. He rubs a hand over his chin stubble. It is his refusing to get out of bed any earlier that ensures he never shaves until work is done.

The boiled coffee nectar is rich and smooth with an aftertaste of bitterness that helps him to inch his way to wakefulness. At least in these first few hours, Natasha's mama and baba, the old woman and the old man, are not around. They are curled up in their sagging bed. This was understandable in the first months of mourning, of course—they had lost a daughter—but as time has gone by, they seem to have forgotten that he lost a wife, too. With their huffs and sighs, it felt as if they were trying to prove that their loss was greater, deeper than his, and they would clutch at each other with silent tears, as if it was some sort of competition. However much he cried, they cried more; however sleepless his nights were, theirs were more disturbed. Until, after the initial shock became a heavy reality, life had to continue and the bread had to be made. But now, it is only he who rises before dawn to keep the bakery running. The old man and old woman's grief still keeps them in their beds and makes them weak, they say.

'We are not so young and resilient as you, Loukas. You still have life, vitality. But for us, our reason to live is gone. It has made us grow old quickly.' The old man's white-stubbled, saggy chin quivered and his age-spotted hand wiped away a tear.

'It will take us time to recover, Loukas, a month or even two at least to get over the shock. You would not begrudge us that, would you?' The old lady hobbled to the sink to get herself a drink of water as she spoke, her stout legs seemingly no longer capable of taking her slight weight even though her clothes hung from her as if she was no more than a wire effigy.

How much of their physical suffering was real, it was impossible to tell, but their sadness filled the house and it only took him a second to think how he would feel if he and Natasha had had a child and that life had been lost. So he told them to take all the time they needed.

That was nearly a year ago and they still lay in bed until the bread is ready to come out of the oven. Ready for the easy job of brushing off the loose flour and blackened bottoms and opening the bakery doors to sell the results of his labour to appreciative customers, the trickle of villagers filtering through the shop door until the shelves are bare.

Loukas drains the last of his coffee and reminds himself that being bitter will not help. He has a job. He has a roof over his head.

'But that's all.' His first spoken words of the day come out rough and gravelly and he clears his throat.

'*Kefi.*' He uses the Greek word for love, life, fun, and the thrill of being alive. 'I have lost my *kefi*.' His voice is less rough this time.

Trying to remember the last time he felt anything alive and happy takes him to places that hurt. Was it when he danced with Natasha in the sand of Saros beach one night when no music played? Maybe it was when she laughed at his teasing, threw a dough ball at him, her baba scowling when it stuck to the outside of the oven, steam hissing from it. Too high to be reached, they giggled away as it cooked and then burned, falling to the floor later as black petals that her mama complained about as she brushed and mopped the floor. Or maybe it was right back at university in Athens. They both felt truly free then, with everything before them, with no thoughts for the economic crash that was going to dictate the course of their lives and persuade them to leave the capital and return to the village. Their friends laughed with them back then. A group of fifteen or so, always someone around to pass the time with. Yes, he definitely had *kefi* then. How easy it is to notice when the joy of life is missing and how seldom when, at the time of having passion, triumph, and spirit, it is taken for granted and consequently it passes so quickly and uncelebrated.

He weighs out the flour, yeast, salt, and water.

'That is the way of man,' he grumbles to himself as he pours the ingredients into the dough mixer.

The weighing out of the ingredients for each batch takes him a full five minutes this early in the morning, his movements still sluggishly fighting sleep. The first dough is now smooth and elastic and he dumps it out onto the table, then pours in the next batch. Once the machine is clanking and rattling in motion, he swiftly cuts the dough on the table into three portions and slaps each into a partitioned trough to rise before starting to weigh the ingredients again. The troughs are lined up neatly, with a clean cloth over the top.

He must not complain. There are many in Athens who have had no work for months. At least he makes enough to put money in his pocket.

'Yes, and in the pockets of the parents of a wife who has been dead longer than we were married.' He grunts as he lifts a sack of flour.

These first few hours of the day are lonely and joyless.

Chapter 2

Ellie's whole body feels soft, stroked lusciously lifeless by the warmth. Something is different. The pink behind her eyelids suggests there is bright light as well as heat. This cannot be home. Remnant dreams still hover but excitement, and just a touch of fear deep in her stomach, pull her awake. Where is she?

The room is unfamiliar. Sunlight streams through the gap in the curtains. The crisp white towel over a chair is not hers. Realisation returns in a rush. She has done it! Really gone and done it, followed the whole thing through, stuck with her half-baked plan. Unbelievable! It wasn't really even a plan-the places of which she dreamed were too unreal. They were where other people lived, locations in bright sun and landscapes soaked in warmth. Everyone wastes time looking at such images on the Internet, don't they? Brief fantasies that, one day, she would be in those tropical places, become the sort of person who travels the world and with that travel, she would find her balance, peace, contentment even. It was a way to fill her days. Harmless. She didn't really think she would do anything about these dreams. Not really. In all honesty, she would probably never have done it if it wasn't for the second bottle of home brew one night when Marcus was late back, again. Presumably staying at Brian's. Again. Maybe it was a knee-jerk reaction, booking to spite him and to show herself that she was worth something, even if he didn't agree or didn't seem to think so.

As she sits up and stretches out her legs, the warmth loosens her shoulder muscles.

She could have cancelled the package holiday the next day, when she was sober and Marcus came back full of hollow apologies. But there was, of course, the secondary motivation.

When the scandal erupted, Ellie gave up her A levels and, as the months passed and she got to know Marcus, it seemed increasingly unlikely that she would continue on to further education. She brought the subject up a few times with him, but each time he found a way to make it clear, without ever saying it directly, that there was no real point in her going back to school and that for now, at least, she must keep a low profile. She quietly tucked away the inheritance from her granny, that had always been earmarked for further education and did not mention the subject again. That money sure as hell was not going to be absorbed into the housekeeping. But a trip to Greece would educate her more than any geography lesson possibly could!

It was also the surprise of the personal welcome email from the hotel owner, a woman called Stella, that made her think twice about cancelling. The way it was worded made it feel exclusive, or intimate, perhaps. Yes, intimate is the right word. It was as if she really cared, as if when Ellie got there, she would be surrounded by friends, which of course was all nonsense and of course she was reading too much into it as usual, but it was the sort of nonsense she really needed to feel at the time.

A seagull screeches outside and she steps towards the balcony door, using her arm across her forehead to shield the glare. She watches it circle and glide on the thermals, its wings outstretched, not flapping.

The truth was, after a couple of days, she had actually forgotten about the holiday. Not completely, just the dates, the reality of its existence. So when she read the email reminder two days before departure, it dried her mouth, made her head spin and caused her to shake ever so slightly. Obviously it was too late to cancel by then and it wasn't something she could discuss with Marcus, so after a couple of hours of consideration, she decided that her only option was to consider it money lost, nothing more. It wasn't as if she had ever believed that she was really going to go.

She lets her arm drop and follows the flight of the seagull as it heads out to sea. It joins other birds and she tries to keep following the one with her eyes, but there are too many. It becomes lost.

The whole day of travelling passed without reality, as if she was not really there but instead was watching someone else. She had not really packed, just grabbed her favourite book, as she had not really believed she was going to go through with the whole thing. The first bus she might have taken anyway, as it went into town. The one to the airport was just to try it out, try and imagine what it would feel like if she was really doing it, with her passport in her back pocket but with no luggage. It wasn't real. Then, suddenly, she was there, looking at a flight information board, the woman on the check-in desk asking for nothing more than her passport to issue her boarding pass. Even that had allowed reality to only return a little. But after the three-hour flight in which she had more than enough time to reflect, she began to panic. At first, she thought it was motion sickness and the air hostess brought her a plastic-lined paper bag, but when she began to feel dizzy, the feelings became all too familiar. Since being caught with Marcus, panic and stress have been her daily companions. She realised she didn't even have the address of the hotel or any idea how to get there. When the plane landed, she moved reluctantly, responding to the physical pressure of the other people around her herding her through passport control, and before she was ready, she emerged into the vast, shiny terminal building. The heat hit her like a layer of silk. The feeling was so amazing that just for a moment, she forgot to panic and part of her believed nothing bad could possibly happen in such a place.

The man said her name with an accent so thick, she did not recognise it as her own. As her name was repeated, it sounded like a chant and she took it up in her mind as a rhythm. It was the waving of a piece of white card with her name on it in hesitant capitals that finally caught her attention. Of course, she booked the meet and greet option, a final twist of her credit card knife into the absent ribs of Marcus. Her relief came out as words, chatter, mindless details of the journey, and it was only after noticing that the driver nodded to all her comments whether good or bad that it began to dawn on her that he spoke no English.

'Is it far?' she asked, and he nodded and smiled.

'Will it take long?' Another nod.

'Are we there yet?' Another nod and more smiles.

After this exchange, she sat silent, wishing she had brought the sick bag from the plane with her as she rested her head against the window. After a while, sleep came over her.

The woman at reception, who introduced herself as Sarah, turned out to be English. She chatted away so easily, so warmly, as if they had known each other for years, allowing some of Ellie's tension and fear to quell. But the normality of their conversation also gave Ellie a reality check on the enormity of what she had done. What on earth would Marcus say? Could she keep this from her parents? But the thought of ringing Marcus that night was more than she could cope with, and sleep again came to her rescue.

The blue of the sea is even more intense than it appeared on the hotel's website, the sands more golden. The sparkling sea hypnotizes her, draining away all her cares until, from nowhere, a dark thought passes through her. She must get in touch with Marcus immediately, let him know she is safe.

She groans. 'Stupid,' she mutters to herself. It would have been so much easier to have left a note. Why on earth had she not done that? He is bound to be cross. No, not cross. He would never be cross. He'll be concerned about why she has done this, perhaps. He will want to understand, be explained to, analyse, and no doubt help her. She half hopes he is cross. At least that would show a bit of passion.

Reluctantly leaving the balcony, she finds the phone by the bed and dials the number. If it connects, he will be able to find out where she has rung from. Does she want that? She replaces the receiver. But won't she tell him anyway? She dials again. It seems to ring for ages. Saturday. The clock on the wall says it is eleven o'clock. What time will it be in England? Maybe he is at Brian's, but surely after she didn't come home last night…

'Hello?' He sounds too calm, and so near. He could be in the next room.

'Marcus?'

'Hey. Where are you then?' He sounds cheerful.

'Um, well, not at home.'

'No. I can see that. Oh, and sorry I didn't make it home again last night, but I did say it might happen this week. Got a bit carried away with re-landscaping around Brian's trains, you know. Plus one too many beers in the process.' He chuckles. 'I know it's not far and I could have walked, but it seemed a long way last night. I would have rung but by the time I thought about it, you would've been asleep. What's for lunch?'

It takes her a moment to think.

'There's a shepherd's pie in the top of the freezer.' She pauses to gain the courage to speak again. 'Listen, it's my turn. I might not get back tonight.' She waits for his response. There is none. 'Marcus, did you hear me?' Silence. 'Marcus?' Maybe the connection is lost?

'Yup, found it. Do I oven it or nuke it?'

'Did you hear what I said? I said I might not be home tonight.'

'Oh. Are you at your mum's then? Best if you warn me of these things really, you know, just so we're on the same page.'

He's so blasé, so infuriating.

23

'No I'm not at Mum's. I'm abroad.'

'Yeah right, good one. So nuke or oven?'

'Seriously. Look in the drawer.'

The drawer under the telephone table is where they have keep their passports and their marriage certificate. She can hear the drawer open, things being moved about, the slowing of movements as he realises her passport isn't there.

'Where?' There is no anger, no concern, just enquiry.

'Does that matter?'

'No, you're right. Space and time are just a concept. Okay, let's try why?' That kind of talk, 'space and time are just concepts' used to impress her not so long ago, back a whole year before she left school. Part of her wishes it still did. Right now, all that impresses upon her is that nothing seems to rile him. Nothing seems to matter.

'Well, I…' is as far as she gets.

'No, it's okay, I get it. I get the "why". You need your space, you need to grow, find yourself, that's why we are here, to experiment, expand, explore. So I guess you can't answer the question of how long, either?' His voice doesn't even register interest.

'Two weeks.'

'Oh, right. Well, I hope you find what you need.'

'Is that it then?'

'Well, it's up to you really, isn't it? What you do with your life. Who am I to demand things of you?'

'My husband! It was you who demanded I marry you.'

'That was different, and I didn't demand. It seemed necessary, at the time.' He speaks disjointedly.

'Was it different, or did it just suit you better?' As the words leave her mouth, her eyes fill with tears. Was that the truth? She puts the back of her hand to her mouth to stop the sob and holds the receiver at arm's length.

'Ellie?'

Putting the phone back to her ear, she breathes deeply, focuses on the room key in her hand.

'Look, it's fine. You needed a break, you've taken one. Don't cry, love. Come on, it's fine.' His voice is softer now.

There is nothing she can think to say, nothing short and succinct anyway, nothing that won't lead to a long discussion or her getting even more upset.

Looking up from the key, the sun outside beckons her. She desires the warmth to touch on her face, melt away her knotted muscles that have returned so quickly.

'Marcus, look, um… I'll call you later, okay?'

The phone replaces with a satisfying click.

She rocks her head from side to side to release the tension. Now that he knows, there is no reason why she cannot enjoy being here. A shiver of anticipation runs down her spine. The view from the window is hers, all hers. Although it would have been nice if he had been just a little put out. He never shows the slightest sign of possessiveness; is that normal?

The view is idyllic, a line of palm trees stretch up into the endless blue sky and beyond them, the sparkling sea in the bay cools the foothills of the mountains on the far shores.

She could easily lose herself in this landscape. Two weeks will be enough time to filter her thoughts. When she returns, she will have a clear head and a settled heart. Everything will feel so much better.

She stretches and yawns noisily. Just being here feels empowering. Her jaw slackens and her head rolls back on her shoulders as she lets the sun coat her face.

The gentle lapping of the sea is just audible, as are the muted sounds of the few early risers talking to each other as they lounge on sunbeds down by the water's edge.

This year has just been one big emotional mess. She has been embarrassed, humiliated, and ridiculed, and things have happened that should never have happened. It will be a lot to mull over in two weeks.

Focusing on the reflecting light on the water's smooth surface, her eyes wash with tears. The beach seems to stretch forever in either direction towards unknown towns, alien places, and just for a second, the world seems a little too big and she forgets to breathe. Maybe that's why Brian's model railway world is so alluring to Marcus—the containment, the control, all so easy.

'Bloody Brian and his railway,' Ellie tells the breeze as she steps back out onto the balcony. Up in the attic, he has a whole world of little trees and sheep in fields by the line, and trains that go round and round. For a boy of eight, that would be fantastic, but for men in their thirties! Why could Marcus not appreciate it but just stick with the car share to work with Brian? Then at least he would be home in the evenings and she would not be alone.

She picks up the room service menu card, which has a smooth beach stone on it to stop it blowing away, and fans herself. She should get dressed.

With the indecision surrounding her departure, she has nothing but her jeans to pull on, which immediately make her feel too hot. Her long-sleeved t-shirt is also too warm. She will have to go shopping, today, immediately.

Sweat gathers behind her knees before she even reaches the door. With her hand on the knob, she hesitates. The breakfast room could be uncomfortable. She knows her fear is irrational, but she dreads that people might stare. It won't be because they know anything. That is ridiculous; how could they? The pictures in the papers were nearly a year ago, and they didn't even look like her. But they might stare just because she is on her own. She's had enough of people staring and pointing and gossiping.

Turing back into the room, she checks out the hospitality tray. Two oat crunchy biscuits and two fingers of shortcake in tartan wrappers. Tartan in Greece! Well wrapped in plaid or not, they will not be enough to hold her until lunch.

The view from her window distracts her again. The sky really is so blue, she could lose herself in it. Blue end to end, not a single cloud anywhere.

Nothing but good is going to happen whilst she is here, she can feel it. This place is going to let her soar!

Chapter 3

'You can't blame yourself, Mitsos.' Stella splits a chicken open with a cleaver and puts it on the well-blackened grill. The sun fingers its way through the open doors and touches everything. The rays reflect off the chilled drinks cabinet, showing smears and finger marks, and highlight the dust-covered layer of grease on the grill hood, adding to yesterday's lingering heat in the small eatery. The sausages sizzle; there is the smell of roasting and fresh lemons. The radio, its knobs and dials covered in plastic wrap, discretely plays *rebetika* music.

'Hey Stella, are you not down at your swanky hotel today?' A man in baggy trousers and white shirt, sleeves rolled up, comes in out of the morning's heat, a lazy smile twitching at his lips.

'I am only here for a second today, Iason.' She smiles at him and shows no sense of haste. He mops his weather-browned forehead with the back of his arm before ducking out of the grill room. One stride takes him through a small door into a relatively dark room with tables and chairs for those who do not want take-away food. A group of farmers look up from where they are huddled around one of the tables and greet him warmly.

'*Yeia sou.*'

'*Ella.*'

A chair scrapes. Stella hears him sigh deeply, and contentedly, as he sits down.

'Beer Iason?' She shouts the question through to him.

'*Nai*, and chicken and chips today please, Stella.'

'Is your son coming in?' she asks, hovering over the grill with extra sausages.

'Not today,' Iason replies. Stella puts the sausages back into their paper packet. 'He is going for a job today in Saros. God, I hope they take him. He is driving me nuts.'

'I hear he runs your home like an army camp since he did his service,' quips one of the other farmers.

'Do you have to stand to attention by your bed?' Another continues the joke.

'It's no joke, my friends. He is running in the hills before any decent man is dressed. He will not drink ouzo with me in the evening because it is unhealthy, and he tells me my cigarettes will kill me!' Iason sighs heavily again.

Wiping her hands down her apron, Stella takes a beer from the fridge. It's early for lunch but some of these farmers have been up since four or five, shooting rabbits for their wives to skin. She cracks off the bottle top with the opener which hangs

31

on a worn bit of string attached to the fridge handle, and takes the bottle through.

'Here you go, Iason. Drown your worries. Shall I open this door?' This room was an independent shop once and has its own door to the street. Stella gives Iason the bottle and then winds her way between the tables. The six farmers could have taken two tables, three if they wanted to spread out but, as is their way, they are crowded around one, chairs pulled over, leaving the other tables marooned, islands, equally spaced across the smooth, brushed and mopped concrete floor.

The pink plastic flower in the blue glass bottle that was on their table has been moved to another, along with the napkin holder and a bottle of water. The ashtrays that have been collected for use at their hub are full. Stella opens the door onto the street and the light floods in, bringing village noises: a car passing, a dog barking, someone shouting at someone called Vasillis, demanding his attention, telling him to get in the house. Outside, on the pavement, a rather thin tree has been wrapped with fairy-lights—Stella's idea to draw more customers. It didn't really make any difference until she put some tables around it. Now, not only does she serve hungry farmers for long lunches, but their wives and children as well in the evenings. It has become the place to go for exhausted housewives, bored with their daily chore of cooking.

But, mid-morning, this outside seating stands empty.

A man passing on a moped parps his horn in greeting. Unmistakable in her sleeveless floral dresses, Stella's thin arms and legs leave the impression that she is nothing more than a child from a distance. But she is far from being a child. Everyone in the village knows her. They know her life, how she has worked, how determined she has been to have all she has achieved and by and large, she is respected. But there are one or two who resent her, call her gypsy behind her back. No one would say it to her face. Stella lifts a hand of recognition to the motorcyclist as she re-enters her eatery.

Specks of dust, unsettled by the opening of the door, dance and swirl, highlighting the divide where sunlight meets cool shade, a diagonal cut across the room. The green walls pale in the light, turning grey where the shadows take over. A framed photograph of a donkey wearing a straw hat is bright in the sunlight, and opposite, a picture of a ship on the sea finds itself in a darkened storm.

The farmers laze, legs outstretched, ankles crossed. Later, they will go to the *kafeneio* and drink coffee, sitting in seats that their babas occupied before them and their grandfathers before that, and make the same conversation as their ancestors did about how the oranges and olives are growing, whether it is a good or bad year for grapes and what unforgivable things the politicians are doing to steal from them and how the men with power will create laws that will make their lives even harder. A game of *tavli*—backgammon—or two will be played, an ouzo drunk, the morning easing into the afternoon until it is time to return home for a nap in the hottest part of the day.

Back behind the grill, Mitsos picks up the conversation as if Stella had not left the room.

'I don't really blame myself but I was the one who suggested we give him a try. He knew that tonight is the official opening, didn't he?' Mitsos uses the metal tongs to turn the sausages. Stella rattles the basket of chips in the hot oil. 'Although I still say that it is foolish to open officially before you have all the correct papers, Stella. You are asking for trouble.'

'It will be fine, Mitsos. We will get the papers one way or another and of course he knew the opening was tonight. If all else fails, one of us will have to serve the drinks tonight.' Looking across at Mitsos, one sleeve of his shirt pressed flat against his side, tucked into his trouser tops, she knows that it will have to be her. Mitsos couldn't unscrew a bottle top without using either his teeth or holding the bottle with his knees, and that's not going to go down well with customers. Not even for one night. Bless him. She smiles to herself. She rests her head momentarily against his remaining arm, which flexes as he turns the split chicken. She kisses his thin bicep as she pulls away.

'Let's use someone we know this time.' Her voice is softer now. 'Experience is one thing but I think if we had personally known this boy, he wouldn't have just up and left without notice.' She lifts the basket of chips out and gives it a shake

34

before pouring the fizzing potatoes onto the waiting plates. 'That chicken ready?' Mitsos springs from his thoughts into action.

'Any ideas?' Stella asks, pouring lemon sauce over the meat.

'Well, who do we know?' Mitsos puts sausages on two of the plates. 'Are you sure Iason's son will not do it?'

'Sure. You've heard he is a strange one. He doesn't smoke or drink, he will not eat anything fried, and he likes to go to bed when it gets dark. He is not the man to run a bar.' She turns her head one way then the other, looking for something.

'Where's the bread?' she asks.

'Oh, he's not been yet.' Mitsos scrapes black bits from the long-pronged grill fork into the bin with the sausage tongs.

'Again! I guess it's understandable that his heart is no longer into it, though,' Stella comments and, as if he has heard them, out from the bakery across the road steps Loukas, a basket of bread in his outstretched arms, his weight leaning back as a counter-balance as he takes small steps across the road.

'*Yeia sou* Stella. Mitsos.' He takes his load down the side of the grill and lowers it to the floor.

'*Yeia sou.*' Stella and Mitsos speak together.

Chapter 4

The dull clonks of what Ellie can only presume to be animal bells drift from somewhere, not very far away, distracting her from analysing the phone call. There are many of them, each with a different pitch. The sound is thrilling, somewhere between being almost too perfect to be true and too exciting to take in. She looks for them beyond the hotel lawns, but nothing is visible.

A couple walk slowly hand in hand to the sun loungers on the beach. A seagull calls overhead as the woman lays down and the man sits on the same sun bed. He unscrews a bottle and pours sunscreen over her shoulders and massages it in, stopping every few seconds to kiss her turned head until finally the woman swivels around to sit up and, with her arms around his neck, they kiss with an intensity that makes Ellie look away. Her stomach grumbles again. She replaces the insubstantial biscuits on the hospitality tray; they are definitely not going to be enough. She needs to do something about breakfast.

There is a light tap on the door.

'Just a minute.' She pulls the bed cover straight and smooths her hair with her hand before opening the door.

'Good morning. Did you sleep well?' It is Sarah, the woman from reception. Why is she here? Why is she knocking on her door?

Ellie struggles to swallow; her empty stomach turns. Has the hotel found out what happened back home, and do they want her to leave? No, that's irrational. She is being paranoid. But then again, she justifies herself, that is hardly surprising.

'I don't start work for another half hour.' Sarah's countenance changes from serene to concerned as her eyes dart across Ellie's face, reading her expression. 'I haven't had my breakfast yet. Do you want to…' She leaves the end of the sentence trailing, her eyes still searching, a slight pucker between her eyebrows.

Ellie's laugh of relief comes out half-snort, half-cough, and her shoulders drop. 'Just a minute.' She hastens to shut the balcony door and grabs the door key and her bag. 'I wasn't sure where breakfast was being served, but I am starving.' In the daylight, she can see that Sarah is a lot older than she appeared last night, older even than Marcus. But there is also something youthful about her, a fluidity, a grace.

'Well, when you arrived last night, I'll be honest, you seemed a little nervous.' Sarah has a hint of an Irish accent. 'It made me think back to when I was first here in Greece alone. It was a bit daunting the first time I ate out on my own until I got to know people in the village.'

It all seems a little over friendly. Ellie can feel her natural reserves, her defences rising, but makes an effort to fight through them.

'So, do you live here full time?' Ellie asks, taking longer steps to keep up. Sarah's strides are easy, her light, muslin dress flowing with her movement. The carpeted corridor muffles the sound of their feet.

'Yes, I do.' Sarah sounds excited by her own reply.

'Is your family here?' Ellie is intrigued.

'No, I came with my husband, but now I am on my own. It's a long story. Here we are.' She steps to one side to let Ellie enter first.

They step into a courtyard in which there are white wooden chairs around white tables with linen tablecloths evenly spaced on the gravel. A circular pond with a small low-level fountain marks the centre of the courtyard, and the stone walls trail with jasmine, bougainvillea, and wisteria. Each table has its own square umbrella to shade it from the sun. Ellie has only seen such places in glossy magazines and television adverts.

'This wasn't on the website!' She tries to remain calm, but her excitement is audible.

'No,' Sarah says, guiding Ellie to the buffet. 'That was Stella's idea. She feels that a surprise makes something more exciting.' It takes a moment for Ellie to connect the name Stella with her welcoming email from the hotel's owner. When she does, she nods in recognition.

The food is laid out either side of them, against the hotel wall, and Sarah takes a basket of bread and a bowl of yoghurt to one of the tables. Four of the tables are occupied. There are two couples, a family of four, and a single man.

'Since I started here, there have been lots of surprises left behind the reception desk. Nothing big, but thoughtful, a bowl of figs, a crossword book in English, a novel that an English guest left behind. She's very considerate.'

Ellie turns to the food. Laid out are honey, feta, fresh bread, dried figs, yoghurt, and wet slices of watermelon sitting alongside cereals and, at the end, toast on a warming plate. With a plate of figs, feta, and fresh warm bread, she sits opposite Sarah. A gecko runs up the wall behind Sarah's head, but she pays it no attention. Ellie is fascinated by its flat, circular toes. It makes a loud clicking noise which seems odd for such a small creature. She wonders if they bite.

The bread tastes as good as it smells, the warmth of it slightly melting the slices of feta cheese. She cannot remember when she savoured anything quite so wonderful.

'The bread's good, isn't it?' Sarah remarks. 'But this is bread from Saros. Stella orders it with everything else for the kitchen. Wait till you try the bread from the village. That is to die for.' Sarah takes her bread and scoops up some yoghurt with the stiff crust. The cheese is creamy, with the slightest tang, and Ellie can taste the olive oil in the bread; she cannot imagine it can be improved upon. Only when her plate is half-empty does she stop to talk.

'I suppose you speak fluent Greek?' she asks, curious to know how someone could make the jump from one country to another.

'My Greek's appalling,' Sarah laughs, and a thousand tiny creases by her eyes appear, suggesting that she smiles a lot. 'So how come you are out here on your own? It's quite unusual for someone of your age.' She puts her coffee cup to her lips.

For some reason, this comment pricks tears into Ellie's eyes. They do not blink away so she tries to use a napkin, pretending it is for her mouth but whisking it across her eyes.

'Oh I'm sorry. I didn't mean to pry.' Sarah is quick. She reaches across the table and squeezes Ellie's hand in a caring, almost motherly gesture.

'No, no, it's alright.' Ellie wipes her eyes. 'It's been a bit of a year for me. Last year, I was taking my A levels. Now I am married and I am not sure what I am supposed to be doing. I feel caught up in a whirlwind. So, I guess I thought that this break would help me make sense of it all.'

'How sensible,' Sarah says, pouring them both more coffee.

It doesn't feel sensible. It feels irresponsible and a bit silly. What does she really think she can achieve, coming here?

'I don't think I was that responsible at your age. How old are you, if you don't mind me asking?' Sarah continues.

'Nineteen.' Ellie's reply is automatic. If she wanted to get away, why didn't she just go to a youth hostel or a bed and breakfast a bus drive away? Why this big, dramatic show?

'Yes, well, at nineteen, the furthest I had got away from home was the Isle of Man,' Sarah chuckles, sounding very Irish. 'And I sure as heck was not on my own.'

'Until coming here, the furthest I had been away from home was Bradford, on the bus,' Ellie replies.

'Wow! So this really is a big deal for you then?' Sarah's voice is soft.

'I think I have made a mistake coming, actually.'

'Ah, you don't know that. Not yet. Anyway, you're here now. Best thing is to have your breakfast, allow yourself to acclimatise a little…'

'Buy some cooler clothes,' Ellie interrupts.

'Buy some new clothes. Good idea!' Sarah grins.

'Are there any shops near here for that kind of thing?'

'You could go into Saros town. That is only a short taxi ride from here.' Sarah leans forward and tears off another hunk of bread and wipes the last of the yoghurt off her plate. 'Or you could go into the village. That's only a short walk, but the only shop for clothes is Kyria Poppy's, and she sells an odd assortment.' Sarah dabs at the corners of her mouth with a napkin and then produces a lipstick. 'Right, I'd better get to work, if you can call it that.' She picks up her plate. 'Go explore; it's fantastic. And if there is anything I can help you with, let me know.' Ellie watches the empty doorway for a minute or two after Sarah has gone before she becomes aware of the other people eating breakfast. None of them are looking at her. The children are blowing bubbles through straws into their fresh orange juice. The single man is hidden behind an English tabloid newspaper. How she hated those newspapers.

Past headlines flash through Ellie's mind. Some of them blamed her as much as Marcus. The spiralling down of her emotions is a familiar, well-worn trail that drags at the corners of her mouth. At least no one knows her history here. She battles with tears. She has it almost to an art form now: breathe and focus, they will dry up in a second. None of it is happening now. Breathe and focus. She is here in Greece and today she will explore the village and buy new clothes.

She is not sure if it is excitement or nerves that ~~drys~~dries her tears as she stands to leave.

43

Chapter 5

On leaving the hotel, Ellie passes across the lawns towards the beach. It is not a long walk to the village and there are several ways she can go, according to Sarah, who recommended either taking the paved road or the path by the sea and then up a dirt track.

'There is a lovely way to walk through the orange and olive groves,' Sarah enthused, 'but you might get lost that way, especially starting from the hotel. You'll find it easily enough on the way back though.' She will try to find it on her return.

The sea is nothing like the briny expanse Ellie has seen in England. Here it is alive with reflections of the sun. When she is close to its edge, looking down through the smooth surface, she can see the sandy bottom quite a long way out, the water is so clear.

Marcus inherited his mother's house, which is by the sea in England, in Blackpool. That's where they went for their weekend honeymoon. At the time, the anticipation of the holiday brought back memories of when she and Mum used to go by bus to Blackpool once a year for a week's break, the week that Father would go to his annual clerical conferences.

Marcus drove them down, hung over and increasingly sniffing and sneezing as they approached. When they arrived at his mother's small and rather drab house, he took himself off to bed, leaving her alone. She was disappointed, of course she was disappointed, but also oddly relieved. Wrapping up warm, she left him asleep and set out on the path to the beach. But when she got there, the tide was out and the beach stretched out as far as the eye could see. She couldn't see the sea, just a huge expanse of wet sand. Her new husband stayed in his bed for the weekend, using box after box of tissues and groaning to himself. So she walked round the town and up and down the promenade in the drizzle by herself. It was not as she imagined a honeymoon would be. The sun came out for a brief hour or two but even then, the sea was still grey and cold looking. It sparkled a bit, but not like it does here.

Looking up from the water near her toes to the far horizon, the blue is staggering, almost unbelievable.

Sinking to sit in the soft sand makes it easier to pull and roll at the bottom of her tight jeans, inching them upward, and once they are halfway to her knees, she kicks off her sandals, slings them over her shoulder, and leaps to her feet again. Walking along with her toes in the water, which is surprisingly warm, a sense of freedom begins to seep into her, a connection to nature and a casting off of the world she usually lives in.

Why has she not come abroad before? Why has she had to wait until now to experience this? All those wet weeks in England, the mist and the cold, when there is this. She stops to look out to sea. She cannot see that this is going to be any part of her future, though. They hardly manage on Marcus' teachers wage as it is and she dare not eat into her university fund again, just in case things change and it does become possible for her to continue her studies, sit her A levels at the least.

Besides, Marcus' idea of a holiday is a weekend pottery workshop. They have been to two already. Originally, the idea excited her; meeting his friends, being part of his life, but the most fun she had at that first weekend was the raku party, which was hardly a party, sitting around drinking homemade wine and stoking a hand-built kiln. There was a bit of excitement when the glowing hot pots were brought out of the kiln with long metal tongs and immersed in sawdust that leapt into flame, or quenched in water that sizzled and hissed, giving off huge clouds of steam. But the thrill of being with older people, being one of them, wore off pretty quickly. All they seemed to do was laze around the fire and chat, drink small amounts of specialist beer, make jokes she could not understand, and fall asleep before midnight. Even Marcus was snoring before she finished brushing her teeth. The second weekend workshop was no better, just more uncomfortable that time.

But this! With her arms stretched above her head, she pirouettes on her tiptoes, which sink into the wet sand. This is perfect. She makes a conscious effort to impress it onto her mind, etch it into her memory in detail, hang on to it.

It is easy to see how Sarah came here and stayed. Came here with her husband and stayed alone. That is a bit more difficult to see. Well, Sarah is a different person. She has not come here for that, rather to make sense of everything, put it all together. But how exactly is she planning to do that? Did she just picture herself tanning by a pool and that this change would remarkably happen by itself? It doesn't sound very probable even if it is possible.

The track from the beach up to the village starts very straight but soon begins to wander, trailing through olive groves, at one point passing by an old barn made of mud bricks. Outside the doorless opening is a plank propped up on breeze blocks to make a bench. Moving closer, Ellie can see names carved into the wood: dates, love hearts, and notches as if someone has been counting off days. It seems strange to find such a display of life in what appears to be an empty barn. She looks inside. It smells cool and there are sacks of cement and builders sand. A new window frame stands against one wall and a thick wooden door is laid along another. It will make a beautiful cottage here amongst the trees. Someone, one day, will be lucky enough to call such a spot home.

Outside, the sunlight filters through the leaves and seems bright by comparison and Ellie squints as she makes her way to where the rough path joins a tarmac road that is cracked with weeds growing down its centre. Here she stops to put her sandals back on and watches a line of ants crossing the road and back. How many are killed every time a car passes? And where are they, all those dead ants? Do they take their dead back to their nest? Everything seems fascinating here. She loves to walk on the moors back home. Trail across the heather and bracken, stay out all day if she could, but the cold usually keeps her moving. It is a rare summer's day indeed that allows her to slow down, lay on the warm peat, and watch the tiny English ants. Here, presumably, there is never a need to hurry to keep out the cold. She can take time to stand still, notice the small things.

Soon the lane joins a main road, just wide enough for two vehicles to pass. Up ahead are one or two low cottages, whitewashed with tiled roofs and plants in painted pots outside. A woman in black wishes her 'kalimera' and stops to lean on her broom to say things in her foreign tongue.

'I'm sorry, I don't understand,' Ellie explains to the woman.

'Den birazi, ola kala.' The woman states and continues to brush off the road outside her front gate.

'Bye.' Ellie trails.

'*Yeia sou*,' the woman replies and waves.

'Ya sue,' Ellie tries.

She is in the village now, and an old man tips his cap to her as he goes into a shop at the corner of what appears to be the main square.

'*Yeia sou*,' he says.

'Ya sue,' Ellie responds. She likes this.

A boy on a moped, who cannot be more than ten years old, zips past, nearly running over her toes. He looks back and grins at her. A donkey being led by a bent old lady is sedately clopping up the main road into the square as if it is the most natural thing in the world. Perhaps it is, here.

Now that she is in the centre of the village, there is so much to take in, she forgets the discomfort of her jeans and long-sleeved t-shirt. A mass of bougainvillaea trails along one wall; a bright coloured canary sings in a cage outside a whitewashed cottage; a dark-haired boy runs along in nothing but shorts, his bare feet slapping on the road's surface. An Asian-looking man lies on a bench at the far side of the square, one foot dangling on the ground, one arm across his eyes.

A palm tree soars from the paved centre, casting a dappled shade over a fountain, and there is a kiosk that gives the appearance that it has burst. On the pavement around it are drinks fridges sprawling away; a freezer, offering ice creams, that reaches towards the road; magazine racks vibrant with colour beckoning the onlooker, and stacks of crates, some empty, some full of bottles, blocking easy passage.

On one side of the small, lifeless fountain, tables and chairs have been arranged, opposite a rather stark-looking café on the other side of the road on the square's top edge. Sarah mentioned this café in her directions. She called it *kafeneio*, a place for coffee and ouzo. Ellie says the word under her breath and treasures it. It was her first Greek word. Now she also knows *Yeia Sou*, which means hello, or perhaps goodbye, or both. She is not sure.

The *kafeneio* is alive, but only with men. They are sitting, standing, laughing, shouting. It reminds her of the ants, but hopefully none of these farmers will be squashed by cars as they pass to go to the kiosk or to sit on the wooden chairs outside on the paved area.

A truck that looks too corroded with rust to be safe on a public road chutters into the square and pulls up. The back is piled with watermelons, and hanging from a metal framework over the tailgate is a large set of scales. The driver climbs out and shouts to the men in the café. One or two stand, hitch sagging trousers, say a last word to their companions, and head toward the purveyor. From the arterial streets that join the square, three or four woman appear, colourful house coats wrapped around expanded waistlines. Some wear headscarves, some have lacquered hair, some wear curlers, two sport slippers.

Once she has taken in everything visually, Ellie begins to notice more. There is a smell of fresh bread, grilled meat and, maybe, some sort of flower or incense.

A man outside the kiosk is shouting at whoever is inside, but after he has shouted, he laughs, the one emotion flowing into the other. How does anyone know who is angry and who isn't? The same pitch of conversation is being had at the café, and they sound like they are arguing, but they are mostly smiling. A giggle escapes Ellie and her neck feels hot. The heat climbs to her cheeks. She is not sure why this behaviour embarrasses her. Maybe she considers emotion is a private thing? To have so much on display seems confusing—but also emancipating. She decides she likes it.

So, if she remembers correctly, at the square she is meant to turn right, then take the first right up behind the bakery. But she is not sure she is ready to leave the square yet and her footfall is slow. Down from the centre, on the left hand side, is another place with tables and chairs outside on the pavement. This one has a thin tree wrapped in fairy lights as its focal point. By the tree is an open door showing a dark interior and next to that are double doors, wide open, and inside, a counter is just visible. From here too voices can be heard, but not shouting, rather talking with animation, perhaps. This place is more inviting than the *kafeneio* and it intrigues her. Her decision to walk towards it isn't one she is aware she has taken until she realises she has missed the right turn before the bakery. There is a small sandwich shop on her side of the road with its door open. On the window ledge is balanced a flat tray half in, half out, displaying croissants and other savoury and sugary items that Ellie does not recognise. She stops to stare.

The talking across the road becomes louder, so she turns. It cannot be possible but she seems to recognise the woman inside, who stops what she is doing and stares back. Then it dawns on her and, before she has thought, she says out loud, 'Stella!' It is the hotel's owner, whose picture is on the website.

'Yes?' the woman replies in English.

She can stay where she is and shout across the road to her or she can take a step in her direction and speak more quietly. Really, she wished she had said nothing so she could continue on her way, but now she is stuck. Looking left and right, she crosses the road.

'Hi, Stella, I am Ellie. I...'

'Ah, Ellie, welcome, welcome, you journey okay? Your room alright? Did you sleep well? Do you need anything?' With this introduction, Stella offers her hand to be shaken and then pulls Ellie towards her and kisses her first on one cheek and then on the other.

'Fine. Good. Everything is beautiful.'

'Oh good. Tonight we have the opening. You are coming, yes?'

There were notices up around the hotel telling of the official opening that night, but Ellie had

53

not paid them much attention, and she is surprised at Stella's invitation.

'It will be very noisy until late,' Stella continues. 'So you have no choice to hear, but come to eat. I will make you a place at my table.' Her manner is so warm, so friendly and relaxed, it catches Ellie off guard and her initial response is to back away, make her excuses. But before she has spoken, Stella takes her hand and leads her to the double open doors with the single word 'Come'. Behind the grill counter, a man with a craggy face and very kind eyes looks up from his work. He is wearing an apron, and in one hand he holds blackened tongs. His other arm appears to be missing, his shirt sleeve ironed flat and tucked into his trousers.

'This is my husband Mitsos.' Stella sounds proud.

'*Yeia sou.*' The man waves his tongs at her.

'Mitsos, this is Ellie, all the way from England, by herself! She will be joining us tonight.'

There is movement to the side of the counter and Ellie and Stella turn in unison. The man there is younger, much younger, about her age even, maybe a couple of years older. He has very short black hair and a dimple in just one cheek as he smiles. Something about him gives her a strange sense that she has met him somewhere before, which is impossible. Looking at him gives her a sense of relief that she is not alone! But that makes no sense. She returns his smile.

54

'And this is Loukas, the baker,' Stella says. He jumps from behind the counter and steps towards her, takes her hand, shakes it gently, and then stands holding it, staring at her.

'Loukas.' He repeats his own name as an introduction in accented English. His grip on her hand is firm and he shows no immediate signs of letting go. His dimple appears and disappears between his smile and his grin. His eyes are liquid brown, his eyebrows drawn straight across, and Ellie finds him hard to look away from. Stella clears her throat. He steps back behind the counter, repeating her name to finish his greeting, 'Ellie.' His tongue curls around the letter *L*.

In response to his intense scrutiny, Ellie wraps her arms across her chest, feeling strangely exposed. She wants him to smile, to see the dimple again.

'You want to come in and sit? Have a coffee? I have farmers to feed but…' Stella doesn't finish this sentence. 'Actually, I will need to go to the hotel shortly, make sure we are ready for the official opening. So I am not sure how much time I have just now. But a coffee is just five minutes, yes?' Stella's invitation to spend time with her is very warming, but she is clearly distracted and there is tension in her voice that is not reflected in her movements.

'Actually, I'm looking for Poppy's shop,' Ellie says and waits to see how Stella responds. She does not want to appear rude by declining the invitation.

'Ah Kyria Poppy. Up by the bakery, round the back, then first lane to the right and you will come across her.' Stella's hands explain as much as her words. 'But you are coming to the opening tonight? I will set you a place on our table so we can talk.'

'Absolutely. Thank you.' Ellie takes a step backwards and tries not to look at Loukas. Her emotional response to him alarms her; she isn't meant to feel anything like this, not now she is married. Making a point of moving away, she confirms 'Up there' in response to Stella's directions and points to the narrow lane by the open doors from which, even from where they stand across the road, the faint aroma of baking bread reaches them.

'Yes, up there. Say hello from me,' Stella says. As Ellie takes her leave, she makes brief eye contact with the bakery man again, quite against her will. The stare he returns makes her blink. Reminding herself that she is married does nothing to quench her feelings. All the parts that are missing in her life, the passion, the care, the companionship, she saw them offered in his eyes. Or did she? Is that really likely or is it more like she just deluded herself with a momentary fantasy?

Chapter 6

First right behind the bakery is a lane lined with single-storey stone houses, years of whitewash icing all angles and smoothing the corners. The roof tiles are all shades of burnt orange and age has moved them, some slipped, some raised, the ridge on one sagging dangerously low in the middle. This one has no doors or windows, and a donkey eyes her lazily from its cool interior. The areas in front of the houses are brushed smooth and washed clean. A cat sits on top of a wall looking at her through half-closed eyes, audibly purring as Ellie approaches but nimbly disappearing over the wall and behind a house as she reaches out to touch it.

Set against the lane, with no courtyard or patio, is a slightly more modern building, incongruous with its straight lines and hard corners. It is not new, but it is not ancient either. Floor-to-ceiling windows with metal frames allow the display of fishing rods, children's shoes, a mangle, an armless and headless mannequin wearing a crocheted 1960s tank top and a pair of sailor's white trousers, creased across the thigh and across the calf, with wide bell-bottom ends. A pair of green waders stands next to four tennis rackets and a pile of half-deflated beach balls, the colours faded along the folds. The door next to the window is open and a smell of incense and damp and old clothes meets her as she draws near. This must be Kyria Poppy's. The feeling of the sun on her forearms and face was bliss on her walk from the hotel, but her jean-clad legs suffered and as Ellie steps into the shade of the shop, the relief is immediate, and for the first time since she arrived, she is glad of her long sleeved t-shirt, as it has just occurred to her that it will have stopped her shoulders from getting sunburnt.

The shop is silent. No one is there. Next to the counter is a deep sea diver's suit complete with brass helmet and weighted boots. It is quite eerie standing there with no one inside. On the floor is a box of blankets, badly folded, and next to that, a pair of roller skates. To her left is a rack of jumpers and t-shirts. The majority of these t-shirts are white, and when she touches them, she can tell they are cheesecloth, the kind of fabric that Marcus sometimes uses to wrap up pieces he is working on, to keep the clay damp. She can imagine that the loose weave will be great in the heat. She pulls at one to find it has embroidered flowers on the front. So hippy, Marcus would love it. She pushes it back into the over-full rack.

'*Ti theleis?*'

Ellie's hand catches a shirt and it falls, only for its metal coat hanger to hook onto one of the other shirts. Her flustered fingers hasten to unhook it

59

and she panics at the thought of how she is going to communicate.

'Er hello,' she stammers.

'Ah English, yes, it was the jeans. I thought you to be Greek. Not many English would wear trousers in this weather but the Greeks, well, they will cover up until late August. Can I help you?' The white-haired old woman has no trace of an accent. She enunciates every consonant and elongates her vowels.

'Are you Poppy?'

'Yes.' The old lady was so dissolved into her chair in a dark corner at the back of the shop that Ellie dismissed her as a pile of clothes. She begins to unfold herself, with no speed, and stands up, using the arms of the chair and puffing. 'Have you been here long? I have a tendency to fall asleep these days. I sit, I think, and then I wake up.'

'That sounds rather nice,' Ellie reflects. Some nights, she cannot sleep at all. In the evening, she always feels tired, she yawns a lot, gets ready for bed, chats to Marcus, he usually kisses her on the nose and then he turns over, his back to her, his arm behind him so she cannot curl up to him and then she lies there waiting for sleep. Waiting and waiting. Just as she feels sleep coming upon her, it is as if she needs to witness the transition and that pulls her back to wakefulness. It goes on all night until she is exhausted. About two months ago, she stopped lying there for three, sometimes four hours. Now she goes downstairs and makes herself a herbal drink and takes it back to bed with a book, by torchlight, so as not to wake Marcus. Once she has drunk her tea and read several chapters, fully absorbing the imaginary world, she can settle down with images of another time, another country. Sleep comes to her then, when she is already far away. But in the morning, it leaves her too tired to get up to see Marcus off to work, so it is usually four o'clock before she sees him, or anyone for that matter, unless she goes shopping or to the library.

"Well, it is and it isn't. I never get anything done these days.'

As Ellie's eyes adjust, the extent of the clutter in the corners is revealed and it is apparent that Poppy is good to her word. Not a lot has been done in the shop for some while, by the looks of things.

'So how can I help you?' Poppy's tone brightens.

'These jeans are actually too hot so I am looking for something lighter. I don't know, a t-shirt and a pair of shorts perhaps?'

'No shorts. That I do know. Not much call for women's shorts. The village girls who are young enough to wear them, their mamas won't let them, and the ones that are old enough to choose wouldn't expose that much flesh. It's a cultural thing. I've some nice dresses though.' Ellie frowns. It feels a bit like shopping with Mother. Why shouldn't she wear shorts? It's up to her to wear what she wants. Poppy holds onto the counter and then grasps the back of a chair and then Ellie's arm to propel her way to a rack near the window. She pulls out a dress in beige and Ellie recognises it as the type Sarah was wearing.

'They're a bit...' She was going to say old for her, but she does not want to offend, 'elegant perhaps? Do you have anything more casual?'

'Well, I have some long, sleeveless t-shirts, but you would have to wear them with your jeans. I have nothing to go with them. I don't suppose you would want a black skirt? I have a lot of call for black. The older women of the village shop here and more often than not, they are in mourning for some relative or other, or a husband long passed. Ahh.' She sighs as if this is the inevitable end for everyone and Ellie shivers.

'Can I see?' Poppy breaks from her thoughts as Ellie speaks.

'What? Oh, the sleeveless t-shirts, yes.' A hand on Ellie's arm, another on the chair, and she is off again from one support to another. Then, as if it is no effort at all, she bends from the hips to reach the ground, pulls one box out of the way, and retrieves a bag with holes in it. Straightening takes more effort.

'Here you go.'

The t-shirts are in great colours, including some pale green ones that are really acidy and a yellow that makes Ellie feel happy.

'Can I try one on?'

Poppy points behind where she was sitting to a navy blue curtain laid over the arms of two mannequins that are pointing at each other. The space is confined; at least all she has to slip off are her jeans. The navy blue curtain is so long, it trails on the floor and becomes entangled in her feet as she tries to take off her sandals. For a moment the curtain, mannequins and all, threaten to fall.

'You need any help?' Kyria Poppy asks.

The combination of the curtain's colour, the enclosed space, and Poppy's question transport Ellie back to a day when the final twist of events reduced her world to a senseless charade.

Her mother wore blue like these curtains. No that's not true, her dress was more of a navy. A dark blue against her long white, netting train, which Mum had held up when she accompanied her into the church hall toilets.

There were no bridesmaids, no flower girls, just the two of them in the powder room. Mum asking if she wanted help with the dress as she squeezed into a cubicle.

'I thought the service went quite well.' Mum's words not quite clear as she spoke without closing her pouted mouth, her nondescript lipstick in her hand.

Ellie lifted layer after layer of the dress as she closed the door. At first, the red stain made no sense. She even tried to brush it off.

Then came the realisation, which tensed every muscle in her body. She rubbed at the stain with toilet paper. The horror of explaining to her father why he would not get all of his rental deposit back brought on her waves of panic. Only after these initial feelings came, like a crushing coil of wet rope, the momentous reality of the bigger truth pinned her to the toilet seat.

'You alright? You've gone very quiet. Do you need any help?' Mum called in her tiny voice.

It took a moment to regain any function. Her vision smearing as fast as she wiped at her eyes, a cold sweat breaking through her foundation on her forehead.

'Darling?' Mum persisted. 'Shall we go?'

There, staring at her from the lining of her dress and on a bit of tissue down the toilet, the reality. No baby. There never was a baby. It must have been the stress that stopped her body from doing what it had done every month for the last year and a half without fail. Normality returned. Normality, but now with a needless ring on her finger.

'Er, Mum, do you have any thingies.' Her voice sounded choked even to her own ears.

'Oh dear, what bad timing, dear. Hang on, there's a machine. I'll just go and get some change from your dad if I can find him. Wait there, dear.'

Thank goodness she had never told her parents about the baby.

Should she go out and put cold water on the dress? Was it too late to explain the situation to her parents? Could she get the marriage annulled barely an hour after the ceremony? Would Dad let her?

'You still there, dear?' The outer door banged behind her mother's return, followed by the sound of coins and a mechanical clank.

'There you are, dear.' Mum's hand appeared under the door, palm downwards, as if to hide the very thing she was passing.

Ellie said nothing, did nothing. Once reassembled, her mother led her back outside, the tell-tale stain hidden behind layers of nylon netting. After a quip from Father about looking miserable on such a wonderful day, Ellie made an effort and pinned a smile on. When she sat at the head table, she leaned toward Marcus to whisper, smile still intact and noticing, for the first time, some grey hairs around his ears. With a couple of words, his world changed, too.

Within the next hour, he became so drunk, he was taken to lay down and he, lucky man, missed most of the speeches about 'forevers' and 'till death do them part.'

'Are you managing?' Kyria Poppy asks again.

'Oh yes, thank you,' Ellie replies.

The t-shirt feels smooth and cool. She hadn't realised how thick the material of her own long sleeved t-shirt was. But the new shirt is absurdly long, almost to her knees. She squirms and pulls at her hot, sticking jeans. The relief at getting them off is greater than she expected. She wishes she could discard her memories just as easily. If the t-shirt looks anywhere near alright, this is a done deal.

'Got a mirror?' She ducks out under the mannequin's arm.

'Oh yes, of course, like a dress. Hmm.' Poppy's head relaxes to one side as she looks Ellie up and down.

'Mirror?' It is just like shopping with Mum.

'Here.' Poppy sweeps the clothes on a rail to one side, behind which is a full length mirror. 'It's good. I like it.'

Ellie is pleasantly surprised by her reflection.

'It's good, really good. You want a belt?' Poppy asks, her head to one side again.

'No, no belt.' Ellie smiles at her herself in the mirror. 'How much?'

Poppy picks up one of the t-shirts and turns it around in her hands. There is a small sticker.

'Five hundred drachmas.' The old woman starts to gurgle, sounding rather like Marcus stirring one of his slip buckets, thick and irregular. The noise grows and it takes a moment for Ellie to realise she is laughing. 'Ah, my!' she manages to says between little bursts. 'You see, nothing gets done.' Another gurgle. 'I have done nothing since 2001. At least since then. That's when we lost the Drachma.' This makes her laugh even more and Ellie finds she is smiling, but she is not sure what about. 'So, let me see, let's say, two euros. Does that sound alright?'

'Two?' Ellie questions.

'Is it too much?'

'No, no it's fine. I'll take the green one as well.'

66

Poppy finds a creased brown paper bag and wraps up the green dress along with the jeans and long sleeved t-shirt.

Outside the shop, the heat hits Ellie like a furnace. She will not be able to stand it if it gets any hotter. Didn't she read in one of Marcus' old magazines that people can go mad in the heat?

Chapter 7

Loukas makes no move to leave the eatery. Instead, his gaze follows the foreign girl as she turns the corner by the bakery and disappears out of sight, and then he leans against the counter to watch Mitsos turning the split chickens, the fat dripping and igniting the hot coals, hissing and sizzling. With only a coffee since he got up this morning and no breakfast, his stomach responds with a gurgle. His dough-clean fingers rub across his belly and catch on the strings of his long white wrap-around apron.

'You want anything?' Mitsos asks, clanging the tongs against the grill to indicate the sausages. Loukas looks longingly, but the old lady will have cooked and will be expecting him back, and he shakes his head. It is beetroot again today.

'Better not.' He tries to hide the disappointment in his voice.

Mitsos casts him an understanding glance, slides the top napkin from a pile on the counter, and with deftly wielded tongs and economy of movement, he takes a sausage from the grill and delivers it to the napkin. He nods at it and looks at Loukas without a word before continuing at the grill.

'So, late again, Loukas? Are you not getting enough sleep?' Stella remarks. Loukas takes a second napkin to mop the juices running down his chin. Stella shifts her hip away from the counter. She heaps a spoonful of coffee and two of sugar into a metal beaker and adds a small amount of water. The stationary electric drinks mixer's metal blade knocks against the beaker's side as she turns it, making talk impossible.

Having finished his sausage, and with no haste, Loukas takes a step through the doorway and calls a hello to the farmers, who greet him back. A quip or two passes as he turns a wooden chair and pulls it to the adjoining doorway to face Stella.

Stella pours the froth of coffee and sugar she has made over a glass of ice and then tops it up with cold water and hands it to Loukas. This event is the daily mark for the end of his working day.

'So what's new?' Stella asks the time-worn Greek phrase as she adds evaporated milk to her own cold coffee, the white curling round the ice as it sinks. Loukas shrugs.

'Nothing. You? I'm surprised you are here. You have the hotel's official opening tonight, eh? I heard the Mayor of Saros is coming and a few more besides?'

Stella throws her head backward, her face glowing in delight. Mitsos stands taller and his chest puffs out. Loukas considers him a lucky man in many ways. 'Yes, the mayor, for all he is worth, but also the whole village, I am thinking.' Stella's face

70

shines at the thought before a small frown creases her brow. 'Everything is pretty much in control but there are still one or two things I need to do,' she adds as her eyes scan left and right, unfocused, and she gnaws the inside of her cheek.

Loukas is glad for her. She went through hell with her first husband. Some of the memories of that time are dim, but others are sharp. He has never mentioned it, but witnessing her pain helped him when Natasha died. It showed him that colder, uglier things can happen. At least his wife left this world unblemished. He can hold his head up in pride at the mention of her name. Poor Stella has suffered so much more in that direction. At the time, it was hard to imagine how her life could reassemble.

Then, through his own tear-filled eyes, he watched Stella transform. All it took was meeting Mitsos, and their love did the rest. They ignited each other, brought out the best in each other. That is what he hoped for when he married Natasha.

How wrong he had been. There was no electricity, no igniting, not even smouldering. Not for him anyway. If only he had recognised what it was that he felt back then, right at the beginning. But he mixed up one feeling for another. There was so much pressure. His degree was going well but there was talk of no jobs by the time he graduated. What he read in the papers about an economic collapse scared him. Then Natasha appeared, offering him whispers from the past. Her attraction, in part, was that she was from his village, only in Athens to study. She represented a link to a time when things felt more sure, to a time when everyone in the village was a relation. When the mamas and *yiayias* of the village ruffled his hair and made him sit and eat their sweet puddings. When the streets were his playground, goats and dogs his friends, and there was less pressure. A lot less pressure.

Even their first kiss was for comfort. It is so easy to see it now. But back then? Nothing was easy to see back then.

That first kiss, the whole evening, it was odd from the moment he returned from his studies that day.

'Sit down, Loukas. We need to talk,' his baba greeted him. Loukas could tell by the look on his face that it was serious. He sat, sweeping his long hair out of his eyes. His mama's hand stroked from one of his shoulders to the other as she passed to take her own chair, lines of worry corrugating her forehead. The three of them faced each other around the table. The highly polished mahogany table that his great-grandparents had bought his grandparents as their wedding present. The matching chairs his *yiayia's* dowry. Softly drumming fingers on the waxy surface provided a release for his nerves.

'You hear what they are saying?' his baba asked. 'But it is not only the change in the economy. The old are dying and the young do not come to us to buy their spices. They go to the supermarkets.' His baba sounded strangely old as he spoke, and that alone felt scary. 'The supermarkets buy pre-packaged rubbish in bulk. Cheap. They do not care about the quality.' His baba did not meet his eye. Loukas had always thought his baba's spice-grinding business old fashioned, the machines cranking and groaning, the air filling with dust, the smells filtering out onto the street. It was obviously not the modern way, and he had been saying so since he was ten, since the first mention of the idea when they moved from the village, but Baba could only see him as a boy. His ideas and opinions were not of the adult world and therefore were to be humoured but not heeded.

That evening of the kiss, he could hear the tension in his baba's voice as he spoke Loukas' own words back to him, and he could see the strain on his mama's face. He stopped drumming and his knuckles turned white as he clenched his fists. His gaze fixed on the picture of the Virgin Mary over the candle in the corner of the room. The house they called home slowly took on an appearance that told him it was no longer a place for him to feel safe. He could feel it, sense it. The whitewashed walls suddenly foreign, the shutters alien. The tiled floor would be someone else's home long after they were dead. Permanence dissolved before his eyes.

'We picked the wrong trade when we moved from the village.' His baba spoke slowly. Loukas bit his tongue in case he was tempted to speak out. 'The raw goods are becoming more expensive each year and the demand less. I can grind the spices all day and all night, but that will not make us any more sales.'

'Right.' Loukas' sharp, emphatic response came because he didn't want to hear any more, nor did he want the temptation of saying anything. He sat there mute, wondering how this was going to affect the fun he was having with his friends. 'Do I have to stop University?' was all he could ask.

He was so much younger then, so self-absorbed.

'No!' his mama was quick to say, her hand reaching across to overlay his.

A chestnut seller on the street called out his wares as he passed the window.

'*Kastana! Kastana zesta!*' Growling on the first *a* and rising towards the end, a wail of a sound that almost lost definition. They waited for his calls to pass, his parents staring at him, Loukas staring at his mama's hand over his until, with a pat, she slowly slid it back to her own lap.

'So what? What are you saying?' he asked.

His baba looked to his mama and then splayed his own fingers on the smooth, warm surface with a faint aroma of spice. He always smelt of spices; they were ground into his palms, etched into the creases, forever present under his fingernails no matter how much he scrubbed.

'Son, I am sorry, but there may not be a business for you to come to after you finish with your studies.'

The news felt like a strange reprieve. It wasn't so serious. He had never dreamed he would slave alongside his baba. Looking at the cracked and worn

74

skin of his baba's broad thumbs, he noticed the ridges of his nails lay in parallel to the grain of the wood, and around his capable and providing hands, there was a slight smudging of the table's daily wax, a smear on its sheen. A bubble of panic formed just below his rib cage, a liquid knot that shook his foundations. It was then that he realised, despite his initial arrogance to the contrary, he had, at some level, been relying on the business as his security anchor, his fall-back. Now, his baba was saying it was going—or even gone!

They sat in silence for what seemed like a long time, listening as the chestnut seller reached the end of the street and turned out of earshot. As Loukas stared, the walls showed their dirt, the shutters clearly in need of repair, the grand table suddenly out of place.

'Well, I just wanted to let you know,' his baba said when at last he stood, his wife by his side, and the two of them retreated downstairs, to the airless, boarded-up, windowless cellar where they ground the spices using the time-worn machine. His mama grabbed her stiff, dust-impregnated apron from the kitchen chair and put it on as she walked. She bagged what his baba ground, using her kitchen scales and a spoon. The edges of her nostrils were always tinted brown.

Loukas sat at the table for a long time. Until that point, thoughts of what he would do when he left university had not really entered his mind. He just presumed there would be a natural progression somehow, but a progression to what, he had never really considered.

He had arranged to meet up with Natasha to go over some coursework later that same evening. But his heart was heavy and the kiss was designed to take him far from his worries, to help him escape. In fact, it left him cold. Her keen reciprocation, however, boosted his ego and it was from this inauspicious start that their relationship was born. The whole relationship was unfair on Natasha and ultimately, it isn't fair on him. But perhaps he deserves that.

'Shall we sit outside?' Stella asks, bringing him back to the present. Loukas returns his chair to the eatery before following her.

'So,' Stella starts as if introducing a fresh topic as they sit. 'What's with the late deliveries? Are you not sleeping?' She wears a small frown, her eyebrows arching to the middle, her concern always genuine. His sigh is heavy and his chest raises and then falls concave; his spine curves into the wooden chair. It is impossible to explain everything.

'You know what you need? A really good night out with your friends, so you laugh and dance and drink and then you will fall exhausted into bed.' Stella stretches out her legs and pulls her sleeveless floral dress smooth over her stomach, which is remarkably flat for a village woman of her age. But then, she never did have children. Mitsos comes out to join them.

'Remind me to order more charcoal,' he says as he puts down his coffee and pulls up a chair.

The sun through the leaves of the tree dapples his face. He moves his chair nearer to Stella and her hand slips over to his knee.

'You know that is impossible,' Loukas says.

'What is?' Mitsos asks.

'I suggested to Loukas that he have a night on the town to cure his sleeplessness,' Stella replies.

'How can he when he has to be up before the dawn?' Mitsos sucks at his iced coffee through a straw.

'I know, but maybe once in a while. He needs to live a little,' Stella smiles.

'I need to live a lot.' The words come from Loukas with such speed and force both Mitsos and Stella turn to him in unison, both their mouths a little open.

'Is that it then, Loukas? You feeling trapped?' Stella's words are soft and quiet.

'I didn't say that,' Loukas answers, but he knows his expression is giving too much away.

'It hardly needs saying, Stella. A young man, in his prime, going to bed before it is dark, getting up before it is light to make an income for his in-laws of a wife that is…' Mitsos bites the inside of his bottom lip. The remaining words hang in the air.

'For a wife that is dead,' Loukas says. It doesn't hurt. Too much. It's just the guilt.

Stella gives a harsh sideways glance to Mitsos, who shrugs as if to say, 'What?'

'It's alright, Stella. She is dead. It's the truth, and so is all the rest of what Mitsos just said. But what to do?' Another sigh expresses his powerlessness.

'If life were easy, we would not notice we were alive,' Mitsos says.

'Speak for yourself,' Stella says. 'I would gladly take "easy" if I had a choice.'

Mitsos puts his glass down quickly as he rocks with laughter, his chair creaking with the movement. 'You? Take the easy way?' He turns to Loukas. 'This is the woman who takes on the eatery single-handed after kicking her first husband into touch. Marries a cripple.' With a jerk of his shoulder, he makes his armless sleeve swing. His voice then becomes serious, the laughter lost. 'And just as her life finds an even keel, she takes on the hotel that is only cheap because it does not have all its legal paperwork!'

Loukas looks from Mitsos to Stella. He has not seen them disagree before. The muscles in Mitsos' cheeks twitch. He seems either angry or scared; Loukas is not sure which.

'The hotel was not cheap because it is illegal. They just didn't know how to get the right paperwork sorted out, that's all. I will sort it. It was cheap because the economy went bust,' Stella defends. 'Besides, you should be pleased. It was your onion field that the Germans were crazy to pay such a high price for in the first place. You should be glad to get your land back.'

'Well okay, but, Stella, really my love, I say again that it would have been better to make it legal before the opening,' Mitsos says, resignation in his voice.

'In what way is it not legal?' Loukas asks.

'Oh, just some planning problem. I just need to speak to the right person,' Stella dismisses.

'You know the old woman's nephew works in the planning department?' Loukas replies.

'That's good to know, Loukas. I might call on you about that,' Stella replies. 'The people I order all the food from for the hotel also have a cousin in that department, so if one way doesn't work, the other might, eh?'

'Did the German firm go bust, then?' Loukas asks.

'I don't think so. But they must have been in serious trouble to take the low offer I made on the hotel.'

'Lower than what they paid us in the first place,' Mitsos says, a little humour returning to his eyes.

'Really?' Loukas asks.

'Sure! They buy my land that was not fit for growing anything, build a hotel, and sell it back to us for less than they paid for the land in the first place.'

'A gift. We would have been fools not to take it.' Stella has the final word with a look at Mitsos that dares him to say any more. She moves her chair a little away from Mitsos, but only so the tree can block the sun's rays from her eyes. Mitsos takes a piece of paper towel from his pocket and wipes the tears of laughter from his eyes with long stokes. He then uses the same piece to mop his forehead.

'Anyway, the hotel is not a difficult thing to run. It is managing the workers that is the hardest bit. Like this barman letting us down. Tonight of all nights. That is the sort of stresses it brings.' Stella loses none of her relaxedness as she speaks.

'What happened to your barman?' Loukas asks.

'No idea. Just got a message this morning saying he wasn't able to take the job. Three weeks he has been promising me that the whole thing was perfect for him.' Stella sucks on her straw, making loud noises as she circles it in the bottom of the glass, getting the last of the froth, ice cubes rattling. 'I've even asked Iason to ask his son to do it, but Iason feels sure the late hours will not suit him. I can't think of who else to ask.'

Loukas shrugs.

They all fall silent.

A tractor grumbles up the street. The farmer waves at the three of them and continues on his way, bouncing rhythmically on his high throne. He has one dog sitting up with him, tongue lolling, and another chasing behind, ears forward, short, fast steps as if he is herding them. A teenager passes on a moped, which he stops outside the corner shop, kicks down its stand, and disappears into the cavernous dark.

80

The village is still until the boy comes out again, jumps onto his moped, and goes back the way he came, driving with one hand, the other holding a blue plastic bag with his purchases.

They sit longer. An old man walks slowly towards the *kafeneio* at the top of the square. It is already busy inside. Farmers use the heat and the need of shade to excuse their games of *tavli* and drawn-out coffees, often with ouzo chasers. It will empty mid-afternoon when the owner, Theo, goes for his *mesimeri*, his afternoon sleep, and the farmers return to wives for their meals. The few that are single or widowed will come to Stella and she will cheer them with her chicken with lemon sauce, chips and sausages before sending them to their homes to rest in the hottest part of the day.

'Well, I guess I will do it myself,' Stella announces.

'Whilst greeting the guests, dealing with the priest, befriending useful officials and organising the food. Yes, Stella, you really love the easy life,' Mitsos chuckles.

Looking over to the bakery, Loukas knows it is time he was back. The old woman will be fussing with the food, laying the table. If he is late, she is not above screeching his name from the doorstep for him to come in as if he was five years old. He would rather spare himself that embarrassment.

He stands to leave.

Chapter 8

Ellie turns back towards the square with a bounce in her step. The dress feels nice, makes her feel her age again. With her parcel under her arm, her attention is drawn by the talk in the *kafeneio*. The palm tree in the square casts dappled shade on its floor to ceiling windows, the glass almost black in the shade, glaring orange in the sunlight. Inside, like ghosts behind the casement, a flux of many white-haired men shift and hover. Trying to see their faces takes concentration. A stone under her foot rolls. She slides. Her arms go out. Her parcel is dropped. Her weight shifts forward. She is going to fall head first. Her hands reach forwards, but they do not meet the ground. Her chin hits something solid. Her chest collides with something unmoveable. She is still vertical. Something has broken her fall.

Initially, it is shock. But then comes pain. Blinking and concentrating on her bitten tongue does nothing to relieve the violent throb. She can taste blood and has lost her bearings.

'*Signomi!*' There is a tone of apology in the deep, warm, foreign voice. 'Oh it is you. Are you

83

okay?' The voice in English is lighter now with recognition.

Blinking again, she gains focus.

The dimple is what she notices first.

'Yes, yes I am fine. Thank you.' He is so close, remaining where they entangled. Ellie tries to back away, to regain her personal space, but his grip remains on her shoulders.

'My shoulder is padded with muscles, but your chin is fragile.' His head tilts forwards, looking down at her, trying to catch her gaze.

'I am sorry I didn't see you.' Ellie's voice is unsure, quiet. His nearness is more uncomfortable than her throbbing tongue.

'Nor I you.'

And then they make eye contact, his lashes thick and dark like eyeliner. Ellie's pain is gone. Her lips part. Her mouth drops open slightly. Something has happened to her legs. They have gained density; too heavy to move, they remain still, locked. Her breathing quickens and a heat from her stomach rushes in all directions, warming and kindling parts of her that normally lay dormant, bringing a second fire to her cheeks. She has not felt like this since the time she was in the store cupboard at school with Marcus.

Loukas is not letting her go, and she has no desire to be released. The look in his eyes is so open, so trusting. His lips so beautifully curved. His dimple so hypnotising. She cannot help that her body leans forward, the distance between them closing a fraction. His hands still on her shoulders; he, too, seems to lean towards her. She can feel his breath now, faint traces of coffee and fresh bread. His bottom lip looks moist, soft. A tendon in his neck grows tight. The stubble of his unshaved chin is soft. His eyes lock hers again and her legs begin to fail her.

'Loukas?' It is a screech that comes from across the square, from the direction of the bakery. *'To fagito einai etimo.'*

'My food is ready,' he tells her in a whisper. It sounds like another apology, and he gently lets go of her shoulders. Some sense returns and her legs grow strength and her feet unstick from the ground.

'Yes, right.' Ellie cannot stop staring.

'I see you again.'

Is it an invitation or a statement of fact?

'Yes, I suppose you will.' The moment she has said the words, they sound distant, as if someone else has spoken them. He is moving away but his eyes are still in hers. She needs to move. Take some control. One step.

'Loukas!' The voice screeches. It is enough. A brief glance into the bakery breaks the bubble and normality returns and he is gone.

'Oh my God!' Ellie mutters to herself as she stumbles into the square.

Loukas only just holds his composure until he's through the bakery and in the kitchen.

'Loukas!' the old lady repeats. The intonation has changed.

His body may not be under his control but his brain is alive and sharp. 'The food smells good.' He hopes that it is enough to deflect her. His heart is still racing. He looks back out of the door to see if he can still see Ellie.

'Yes, you may well check to see who has seen you. The whole village could have seen you! And your wife, my only daughter, not even cold in her grave these twelve months.' The old lady's high-pitched voice hits him like cold water.

Loukas' heart crashes back to reality. The smile that is pressing his cheeks drops and is replaced by a hot flush.

'You might well blush. Has your love for Natasha faded so quickly?' she continues, her eyes filling, her hands beginning to tremble.

She dumps knives and forks on the table with a clatter and scrabbles in pockets and sleeves for a hanky.

'What's going on?' The old man enters the room through the back door where he must have been stacking wood, bark clinging to his hair.

'Ask Loukas. Ask him how well he loves Natasha and let's see if he can lie to your face.' The old lady is crying now, uncontrollably.

'Steady on my love, of course Loukas loved our girl. How could he not?' His usual bent stance straightens and he is lithe on his feet to cross the room and put his arm around his wife, all signs of the frailty of age gone. A fleeting thought crosses Loukas' mind that this is odd. Surely age and creaking bones do not come and go on a whim, but he chases this away as uncharitable.

'Tell him, Loukas, if you are not shamed to silence.' The old woman nestles into her husband's arms, sniffing loudly, the mucus inhalation audible.

'It's nothing. There was a girl outside. We bumped into each other. She wasn't looking where she was going and neither was I.'

'She was in your arms and on our doorstep!' The old lady's voice loses neither its pitch nor its volume amongst her tears. The whole village will have her views of things if she carries on.

'She fell, I caught her by the shoulders. She was not in my arms.' Loukas is partially annoyed by her intimations but mostly horrified that denying the embrace, the embrace that never even happened, feels as if he is denying his right to breathe.

'Who was it?' the old man asks calmly but his jaw muscles are tense.

'No one.' The words dig under his ribs, feeling like a lie. 'Someone staying at the new hotel, a friend of Stella's.'

'Might have known that gypsy tramp had a part in this,' the old woman spits.

'Steady on.' The old man leans away to look at his wife's face.

'Why are you speaking badly of Stella?' Loukas' eyes widen.

'Ach. You do not know her like we do. We were at school with her. Her mama was the same. Married a good man for what she could get.' The old lady has gained momentum now and makes no attempt to quieten this new defamation.

'I think you are going too far,' Loukas defends, but this is all coming out of the blue. He is not sure he understands. He looks to the old man.

'It was different then, Loukas, you have to understand. Gypsy stayed with gypsy. It was unusual, shall we say, that Stella's mama married a Greek man.'

But Loukas cannot hide his disgust at this new direction the conversation is taking. 'What on earth has what Stella's mama did got to do with Stella, and why are you attacking Stella when it was Ellie who I bumped into?'

'Ellie is it? Not even a Greek girl,' the old woman hurls.

'This is unbelievable.' Words fail Loukas. The old man breaks from holding his wife and steps toward Loukas.

'Stheno, my love,' he addresses his wife. 'I will take Loukas for a coffee. We will eat when I get back.' His wife nods in approval, as if her will is being done.

'I don't want coffee,' Loukas protests.

'Come, we drink coffee, we talk like men. Come.' Taking Loukas' elbow, he steers him through the shop to the street.

They cross the square in silence. No signs of age have returned to the old man's legs. What is it then that keeps the man in bed in the morning? Is it his aching limbs or plain laziness, and why are these things coming to the surface now? Or is it that he is only just noticing now? Loukas enters the café first, under the curling curtain of cigarette smoke that hovers above the coffee and ouzo drinkers' greying heads.

A dozen conversations drone in a continuous hum, speckled with bursts of laughter, occasional coughs. The high-pitched clack of wood on wood as pieces are lazily slammed on battered backgammon boards by two men who battle out their game.

The large room is sparse with no adornment, nothing of which care needs to be taken. The floor is painted a light grey and the walls, once a stark white, are yellowed with age. The paint on the stretchers and top rails of the chairs has worn through to the wood by hand and foot. The circular metal tables on curved tripod legs have paint-chipped edges, but their construction remains solid, practical.

The number of men has reduced since mid-morning. They all have their routines, their wives to which to return. The old man points at a table in the corner, away from the cluster of remaining men. The café owner, behind the counter, finishes swilling a glass and, with a light step, attends them at their table. He has frizzy, salt-and-pepper-coloured hair that sits like a halo and bounces as he walks, and continues to move even when he has come to a standstill.

'Two coffees please, Theo.'

'One,' Loukas growls at Theo but realises he is growling at the wrong man and makes an effort to soften his tone. 'Just one please, Theo.'

Once Theo is bouncing back across the room, Loukas turns to the old man.

'So? What on earth has Stella and Stella's mama got to do with anything, and why is the old lady suddenly so cross at her?'

'Ah, Loukas, you were married for such a short time. Not long enough to know women.'

'What is that meant to mean?'

'Listen my boy, they are not logical like us. They think a thought and they hang on to it forever. You would have learnt this with time, even with my sweet Natasha. But if we stay here for a while, Stheno will calm down.'

'Well whatever the old woman's issue is, it has nothing to do with me. But it's not right to speak like that about Stella. She's our neighbour. We do business with her. She is my friend.'

'She's your friend is she? Then tell me why she does not order the bread for the hotel from us?' The old man asks quietly.

Loukas cannot answer. He vaguely wondered when the hotel first tentatively opened its doors but the thought has not occurred to him since. It would be a big order, too, and would make a difference to them.

'Listen, we are the old generation, me and the wife.' The old man straightens slowly as if to emphasise his aching bones but to Loukas, the pantomime is wearing thin. Loukas is beginning to feel unsettled about the old man's plea for rest in the mornings and he is beginning to wonder more and more if all this time, they have been taking him for a fool, playing on their age, and, God forgive, the death of their daughter. But why? Just so he will make the bread instead of them? The old man interrupts his thoughts.

'In our time, in Greece, there were only Greeks and very few Albanians and Romanians and all those types of people mixing in. When we were children, we had never seen a black face but now the Africans are selling cheap watches and jewellery in all the bigger towns and the Indians and Pakistanis help us to pick the oranges. It is a different time.'

'Are you going to lecture me on racism?' This is ridiculous. He lived from the age of ten in Athens, went to university there. He lived a cosmopolitan life until university ended and he and Natasha decided that a job at her family bakery was better than no job at all.

'No, no son. I am just telling you that some people, Natasha's mama for one, finds it hard to let go of the old ways. To her, the gypsies and Albanians may as well be one and the same and she believes both will murder her in her bed, given the chance. They are not Christians, you know? They lie.'

Loukas' face feels on fire, his fists tighten, but his imminent explosion is halted by the arrival of the old man's coffee. After a few pleasantries, during which Loukas regains his composure, Theo leaves and the old man continues.

'Before you say anything, Loukas, let me tell you one of the most popular tales we would tell when we were even younger than you. There was no television then, remember. I first heard this from...' He stops and looks up to the ceiling, trying to recall. 'Well I can't remember who first told me it, but it went round and round, people telling it backwards and forwards. They said it was true, and who knows maybe it was, but I think there is no smoke without fire.' His takes a sip of coffee. 'So here is what happened. A farmer from across the bay,' he twists his hand and his thumb loosely indicates the direction of the sea, which is just a short walk away but hidden by a hill, 'needed help with the work in the fields. At the time, his wife had not borne him children. Anyway, an Albanian turned up at his gate and the man employed him. The Albanian works hard and he is paid and he goes away. The next day, he came again and then again the next day until he becomes as one with this man and the work that needed doing. All this time, he had been sleeping under the trees. Winter comes and he is still sleeping under the trees, but he does not complain. In the spring, the farmer's wife falls pregnant and in time, they have a son. Well, the farmer has grown close to the Albanian working alongside him day after day

92

after day.' He stops to take another sip of coffee, raises his cup in greeting to a neighbour sitting a few tables away and calls 'Yeia mas.' Another sip and he continues.

'So he asked the Albanian to be his son's godfather. He had grown so trusting and fond of the man. The following winter, he allowed the man to sleep in the house when it was too cold and the Albanian thanked him for this. But one day, suddenly the Albanian said he was leaving. He had made the money he needed and must return to Albania to be with his own wife and children. The farmer was sad to see him go but drove him on his tractor to the station. They stood side by side at the station and it is then that the Albanian said, "Costa", he said, or whatever his name was. Let's say it was Costa. "Costa", he said, "you have been a good and kind man to me. You have given me work and entrusted me to be the godfather of your child. But you are a fool." "Why so?" said the farmer. "Because", replied the Albanian, "for the all the nights I slept in your house, if I thought you had so much as a hundred drachmas on you, I would have slit your throat as you lay sleeping and been away before it was light".'

The old man pauses for breath and effect. He does not seem to be satisfied with Loukas' response so he explains, 'A hundred drachmas back then was probably about ten euros now. So for ten euros, this man would have slit his friend's and his friend's wife and baby's throats for that mere trifle. And this is

93

from the mouth of the Albanian, mind you. The farmer was not saying it himself.' The old man leans over his coffee and takes another sip.

For a moment, Loukas stares, struggling to form what he wants to express. 'But as you were so keen to point out before you started this story, they are all liars! The foreigners. So why choose to believe this?' Loukas finally explodes.

'Why would the Albanian tell such a lie?'

'It is a story, old man! It is not from the mouth of the Albanian; it is from the storyteller's mouth. Propaganda!'

'No, no, son. These stories were tales of what was happening around us back then, from one person to another.'

'Twisted by the teller for a better response, time after time. It is nonsense.' Loukas looks out of the windows, shaking his head, slowly wondering why he is even in the village anymore. Natasha is dead. Why has he not gone back to his family in Athens?

But he knows the reason: things are worse now in Athens. There is no work to be had. That, and the guilt is still there.

*

Chapter 9

Ellie has no idea where she is going. Mentally, she has not been released from his grasp, his hands still on her shoulders, her eyes locked on his. Her legs move automatically, one foot in front of the other. Bearing neither left nor right, she walks straight across the square and then up a narrow lane flanked either side with stone walls. Those lips!

And how magical it feels. Thousands of miles from home, the sun's heat that permeates her bones, the dry earth, the sparkling sea, all of which turn common events, like bumping into someone, into a dream. A wonderful dream.

But she should pull herself out of this fantasy. Marcus is, after all, at home waiting for her. Marcus! A shiver runs down her spine, which causes her eyebrows to raise. She has never had that reaction to the thought of him before. A touch of sadness maybe for what they once had, and, if she can bear to be honest with herself, it really was only the once, and so quickly lost, but never a shiver. The tremor seems to have something to do with his age. It's ironic, as his age was part of the attraction originally. It certainly attracted Penny Craig and Rebecca Slater before her. The thrill of him being their teacher.

Loukas' skin was so smooth, tanned. His sleeveless t-shirt and wrap-around apron crisping his outline. When he held her, his shoulder muscles showed strata and there was a dip between his shoulder bone and that muscle that goes from his neck into his back. So deep, she could have drunk wine from it. Marcus' skin is slack; he is not one to exercise. In fact, he no longer even kneads his clay like he did back at school. She can almost smell the art room. The gum and glues, the damp clay, traces of school dinners.

Penny and Becky giggled as Marcus' dexterous hands worked and pushed the lump of clay into a rhythm. He generally had a routine in their lessons. The majority of the kids working at their own project were left to get on. But Marcus would start the kneading on their table, get their attention before cutting and slapping it into round balls and then slipping onto the seat of the wheel. He would kick it into gear like it was a motorbike and throw the clay so adroitly into the centre of the spinning disc. Then Penny and Becky would huddle closer together, excluding her, whispering behind cupped hands as Marcus sprinkled water onto the clay and drew it up into a tower, wet and smooth, before pushing it down flat again. The liquid and the earth turning to a slurry over his fingers.

'Smooth strokes,' Marcus explained. 'Even pressure and smooth strokes.' Penny and Becky giggled. 'The idea is to release any trapped air pockets. It's all about release.' The girls' giggling increased.

Ellie didn't really get it back then, not totally. She would feel more sure what she was thinking was right if someone would confirm it for her.

'Penny, you know when Mr Cousins throws his pots?' Penny started to giggle even before her question was out that break time. Becky joined in.

'Listen El, if you don't get it, you don't get it. It's not something that can be explained.' 'I think Ellie's a bit of a "late bloomer", as my mum would say.' And the pair huddled together, excluding her again.

'Slow, more like.' Ellie looked up to see a boy who was always hanging around with Becky and Penny. As he passed, he made prolonged eye contact with Becky, who grinned in return, her head turning to watch him swagger down the corridor, jumping to touch the light bulb halfway along, looking back to check if Becky was still watching.

She didn't really know what 'late bloomer' meant either back then, not fully. She does now. Now she can see she was a bit young for her age maybe, certainly not as advanced as those two, but then with her father being a vicar and no television or Internet allowed in their house, let alone mobile phones, it wasn't really surprising. How much she has learnt in this last year!

The biggest mystery back then was when Penny and Becky went into the store cupboard with Mr Cousins, as she knew Marcus to be then. She only had a half-formed idea as to what, in the store cupboard, could cause so much laughter. There was one obvious thought, but surely they weren't doing that! But then, why had she not been allowed in too?

She felt she had purposefully been left out that time, but she always felt a bit left out, really. That was why, when it was her turn to be invited, she went into the store cupboard with him, too. Only she was on her own that time.

The lane Ellie is on is climbing now. The tufts of what once would have been grass up the centre are burnt brown and dried with the sun. Either side, the white stone walls are thick with years and years of paint and have no edges. They are smooth as though they are made of clay. To her right is a gate with a wooden crate or something fixed to it as a letter box, its sloping roof made out of the front of an old drawer, the metal handle that is still attached glinting in the sun. By the stone gateposts, the dried grass is longer and has crumpled to the ground. Something small rustles in its cool shadows. Ellie's hands come up to cover opposite shoulders. She is burning, but it is hard to care as the warmth of the sun on her skin is so sensuous.

She keeps climbing until the lane peters out and pine needles cover the barren earth under the trees that crown the hill. The tops of the trees hiss quietly as if unfelt breezes stir them. Her footfall is cushioned and there is a hush, only the occasional buzz of a bee passing her. It is the perfect place to sit. The view of the village below her, the distance diminishing the houses to a toy town, the people to insects. Beyond the village, the plain stretches until it becomes misty with distance and shimmers in the heat and, far away, what could be a mirage of purple mountains. The regimentally lined orange and olive groves patchwork the plain's entirety. Handkerchiefs of order laced together to blanket the earth down to the sea. It is like something out of a book, or one of the *National Geographic* magazines that Marcus collects. The ones that date back nearly twelve years to when he was twenty, as he has proudly told her.

Loukas won't read anything like the *National Geographic*. He will read a music magazine, or something about bikes. He probably doesn't have time for reading.

But the image of him distorts as she remembers his eyes rimmed with dark lashes, his muscular shoulders. The chances are, someone with his looks will be like one of those boys who laughed along with Penny and Becky when the whole Marcus thing kicked off. School felt so hostile, an emotional minefield, no matter how carefully she trod. If someone had asked her before the event, she would have said it would have made her really popular. Penny and Becky used to joke and brag about their store cupboard 'ordeals' in the sixth form common room and everyone would laugh or pretend to be shocked. So why, when she did it, did they just stare at her? The boy that hung around with Penny had the audacity to ask her if she knew what she was doing. She had thrown her head back and laughed. How stupid did they think she was?

Stupid enough to not really know what she was doing at all until it was too late and stupid enough to get caught, was the answer. If it had been Penny or Becky they would have turned it around and it would have been put across as daring or brave or grown up or something. But it was Penny and Becky who delighted in asking her what possessed her to go so far. They, after all, had only teased, played like they were going to but then left the silly old man hanging. Pervert that he was. What was she thinking?

Here, with the pine trees wrapped around her, blanketing her from the world, the sun kissing her forehead and the whole world at her feet, she allows the thought that has been coming and going recently to rise to the surface. Did she do the wrong thing in marrying Marcus? Did she ever have a choice?

Ellie recognised the boy who opened the storeroom door. He was not in her year, but his mother arranged the flowers at church. It was not long before the news spread all over the school.

She returned home that night terrified of the ordeal that awaited her. They wouldn't give her the chance to explain her side of the story. Certainly

Father would be quick to condemn. But there was an eerie silence as she walked through the door. She waited for Father to start as they sat down for dinner, but no words came. Her initial thought was that they were too angry to speak but after the first course, it occurred to her that they didn't know.

They finished dinner and she was washing up, Mum drying when Father went to take a phone call in the hall. He never spoke loudly on the phone, always as if he was talking to a bereaved parishioner—hushed, soft—and this time was no different.

The click of the receiver as it was returned to its cradle sounded louder than normal, his step across the hall more deliberate. He stood in the kitchen doorway waxy faced, stiff limbed. Then he exploded.

'For the love of God, Ellie, have we not brought you up better than this?' Ellie rinsed the plate slowly, her wet fingers creaking across its surface, making her teeth jar. 'He is your teacher, for God's sake.' His words lost their enunciation as his wrath grew and Ellie picked out fragments. 'This behaviour … inappropriate … Immoral …'

When she could bring herself to look at him, all she could focus on was the spittle on his lips and the white flecks in the corner of his mouth. His face was bright red and she felt hers drain white. She was going to faint and he was going to explode. The whites of his eyes glowed, bloodshot, she picked out the word 'congregation'. She always seemed to come second to his congregation. Mum stood quickly to take his arm, stroking, soothing, imploring him to calm down.

'Remember your heart condition,' she implored of her husband. 'Tell me dear, tell me calmly. What has she done now?' Ellie slumped, hearing Mum talking as if she were not in the room.

Father whispered into Mum's ear the things that had been told to him on the telephone, which were too sinful to speak out loud. As he hissed his words, Mum's face drained ashen, her eyes widened, her mouth dropping open. With quick movements, she patted Father's hand, her eyes darting across the carpet and back. Finally she cleared her throat.

'Right.' Mum's mouth was a thin, tight line, the skin under her left eye twitching as she commanded attention. 'I have no doubt, no doubt...' Her voice was quiet but her words clearly emphasised. 'That there will be no fuss.' She looked from Ellie to Father. 'No fuss,' she repeated so quietly, both of them leaned towards her slightly, straining to hear her. 'Mr Cousins, Marcus,' she corrected herself, 'will have good intentions. Marriage will be...' The two words drawn out, accompanied by hard eye contact with them both, 'the next step. He will come round to tea and, if necessary, I will have a word.'

Father's shoulders dropped and the colour slowly returned to his cheeks.

With that, normal life at home resumed, almost. Conversation was reduced to close-lipped minimalism, evening prayers were extended, and a bible was left open by Ellie's bed with passages highlighted. Decency would be restored by the force of Mother's will, with Ellie as the sacrifice.

Then there was the scare.

'Oh…' Under the pine trees, Ellie searches for a swear word, one that's not too bad but will still express her feelings. 'Bugger!' she finally ejects.

The scare was the final blow. In her year, everyone seemed to be relishing the whole incident and she even started to get funny looks and whispers behind her back from the younger kids. There was gossip about Marcus being pulled up in front of the head and, after a few of days of his absence, it was on everyone's lips that he was suspended from teaching 'until further notice.' There was talk of the police being brought in. Some of her classmates looked at her with pity, and others just sniggered. Penny and Becky created the biggest distance they could from her, playing down their history of exchanges with Marcus and focusing on her. She felt very alone.

The scare came only days later, when she found she was late. For three days which felt like a lifetime, she waited, told no one, and, then, she used a public phone to call Marcus. He was not pleased to hear from her and almost sounded like he was blaming her for his suspension. But she managed to persuade him to meet her in the public library in Bradford.

'You'd better have a really good reason for this,' he greeted her. 'If I'm seen with you, I will never be able to sort this all out.'

For some reason, she thought it would be easier to tell him face to face, but the laughter that always showed in his eyes was not there and his sideways smile was nowhere to be seen. He was unshaven and the square of his jawline was hidden in a greying, prickly-looking fuzz.

'I have. We have,' was all she managed.

'Well?' He began to run a finger along the spines of the art books as if that was more interesting.

'I think maybe three of us have.' Clumsy, but none of the right words would come out of her mouth.

'Three?' His forehead lowered over his eyes, which darkened.

Her lips sealed shut. If she said anything else, she would cry. Her left hand lifted to rest and rub circles on her flat stomach. His brow lifted and his eyes grew wide at this, and the horror that contorted his face before he took control said it all. With rigid arms rustling against his jacket, he disappeared down the Art History aisle. After a slight delay, she followed, but he wasn't there. Nor was he in the Fine Art section or in Modern Sculpture. After a couple of minutes of weaving between book cases, she slumped at one of the central study tables, where she wept silently. She had been crying for what felt like an age when a man with steel-framed glasses, a whole table away, looked up from his thick leather-bound book and glared disapprovingly. She had no one to turn to in the world.

'I will tell the head we are marrying.' The whisper in her ear was so unexpected, she jumped. The bespectacled man on the other table demanded hush, but she didn't care. Marcus had come back! Her heart soared; she was not alone. The thought sent a thrill through her, the happy-ever-after promise of every film she'd had the luck to watch in the church hall could be hers for the taking. He wanted to marry her!

'That will put the end to the whole thing. It will stop the press, the police, your parents, and the gossip. Besides...' He leaned in. She thought he was going to kiss her and she parted her lips but instead a hand came up and took hold of a strand of her hair. 'You know how I feel about you.' He then tucked the piece of hair behind her ear. They agreed to stay silent about the child before the wedding, and he patted her shoulder before he walked away.

The following Monday, Marcus marched into school. The news swept through the corridors and sixth formers on free time lingered in the hall as near to the headmaster's office as was allowed. Half an hour later, news of the wedding rippled through the classrooms.

Then the headmaster rang her father and congratulated him, much to the poor man's surprise. After the initial shock, a hush came over the sixth form common room and they witnessed the events as they unfolded, mostly in silence. It had all got far too adult and civilised to be of any real interest to them.

There was an 'I hope you know what you are doing?' from Penny and 'At least he's a good kisser', from Becky but after that, everyone pretty much left her alone. Very alone—she no longer had anything in common with any of them. They moved on and left her behind.

A few meetings with Marcus followed, arranged by Father and in very public places. During one of these, Marcus said that the attitude to him by the school board had changed and that they were thinking of lifting his teaching suspension if the wedding could go ahead soon. Father seemed equally keen to get the whole thing over with. Marcus showed no interest in dresses or flowers and would have had a registry office wedding if he could have. But that could not be, not with her family. So they hastened down the aisle before anyone knew of their fears. Then there was the incident in the toilet where life turned into a charade. The reception became a joke. Afterwards, they were driven to a bed and breakfast for their first night as man and wife. Elle cried. Marcus continued what he started at the reception and got even more drunk until he fell asleep in a chair in the bay window.

The next day, they drove to his mother's house by the sea.

The following Monday, the school asked Marcus to leave anyway. The problem was that whilst they had been away, the papers got wind of their misadventure and the fact that they were now married made no difference—if anything, it fuelled the story. In short, they were having a field day, and a throng of reporters greeted them at the entrance to Marcus' flat when they got home. Marcus drove straight past. Ellie suggested her parents' house, but they were there too. In the end, they booked into the bed and breakfast again but the owner must have rung someone as half an hour later, there was a knock on their door and they opened it to flashing bulbs and a barrage of questions.

Finally, they retreated to a house belonging to a friend of Father's who happened to be on holiday in Bermuda. Marcus refused to go out at all and so, alone for a few days, Ellie played dodge the reporters as she was, inadvisably as it turned out, still trying to finish her A levels.

Some really horrible pictures where printed in one of the national papers. One where she had her cheeks full of her lunchtime sandwich and another one where she was blinking so she looked like she was challenged. At the advice of the headmaster and her father, she stopped going to school after that.

In the end, with Marcus having no work and Ellie no longer at school, the sensible thing to do was to move away. Go somewhere they would not be known.

Marcus applied for teaching posts and took the first job he was offered, in a town on the other side of the moors. It took an age to drive there, along narrow, winding lanes, but as the crow flies over the moors, it was just a good stretch of the legs away from where Ellie grew up. It was a one-street village, lost in time and hidden in a dell, which Ellie had always liked the look of. She often used it as a destination to walk to in her solitary moor walking days, before the whole Marcus thing happened. So the move there didn't seem so bad.

The best thing was she was free of her hometown gossipers, abuse throwers, and church sympathisers, as well as her family. She wore her hair up and her hat down. Marcus was out at his new school every day. His new headmaster was a liberal man, a non-conformist at heart but he suggested to Marcus that Ellie continue to keep a low profile for a while longer whilst Marcus got established at the school, made some friends, and it was not long before she began to feel isolated and lonely.

'Bugger and damn and poo.' Ellie hugs her knees and rests her head on top, thinking she is going to cry until she catches the edge of the damage to her tongue against her teeth, which reminds her of the collision. Lifting her head, she looks out across the land. It gives the impression that she could go in any direction she wanted and get lost in seas of foreign experiences and waves of alien cultures forever. All her fears of being on foreign soil seem to have gone.

Maybe that's progress?

Chapter 10

'Come on, son. Let's go eat.' The old man throws some coins onto the table.

'I am no longer hungry.' Loukas does not stand when the old man does.

'Suit yourself.' And with a nod to Loukas and a wave to a few of the men left in the *kafeneio*, he makes his way into the sunshine and hobbles to the bakery. The signs of age are back, his progress not so fast. Everyone except those playing *tavli* watch his progress. There is little else to do.

Once the old man is in the bakery and the door is closed behind him, Loukas jumps up, kicking the chair in his haste. He grabs at it to stop it falling, replaces it gently, thanks Theo. He dithers before descending the three steps onto the road and then sets off with long, purposeful strides across the square.

'I'll do it!' he announces.

Stella lowers her chin and looks under her brow at him, her eyes narrowing.

'Do what?' Mitsos looks up from the grill that he is now cleaning.

'The bar tonight. I'll do it.'

111

Stella says nothing, but searches his face.

'Really? Do you know how to mix drinks? What about the bread?' Mitsos cannot hide his relief and his questions sound almost as if he doesn't wish to have them answered. He drops the cloth he is using and leans the poker against the counter. Loukas has his full attention.

'I had a job in a bar in Athens when I was at university there.' At the time, he resented the work, but is glad now that he has had the experience. It was in his last year of studies and money had become tighter more quickly that his baba had predicted. As a result, it was either work or leave university. There was a pressing need for him to contribute to his fees as well as to help put food on the table. A small, cheap table though, not the mahogany one, which had been sold by then, along with the chairs.

He turns to face Mitsos.

'As for the bread, maybe tonight I only get a couple of hours sleep, but maybe Stella's right. Maybe a change, a little less sleep one night will make me rest better the next night.' He is going to do this whatever the cost. Damn the old woman and the old man! They survived before he came along and they can survive one night now if need be. His anger is mixing with excitement. It's funny how he can almost feel his dimple from the inside when his smile is big enough.

Stella still hasn't spoken.

'Stella?' Mitsos asks.

'For one night?' She says it as a question but Loukas can hear that it is a command. He understands. It is a small village. If the bread does not get made because of her hotel then there could be knock on effects, maybe fewer farmers at her eatery, the ripple of gossip. He knows and loves all the villagers, and is related to more than half of them, but even so, they can be very petty at times compared to the Athenians.

Also, Stella will not want to have any open argument with his in-laws. As for his own thoughts on the matter, first and foremost, he wants to protect Stella from the acid views of the old woman and secondly, where else would Stella get her bread for her eatery every day if she is on bad terms with her neighbours? No, it is important in a community such as this to tread softly.

'Yes, Stella, not to worry. For one night, and the bread will get made,' he promises.

Chapter 11

Being in a warm country has a unique effect. Look at Penny when she went to Dubai and Becky after her trip to Florida. They came back with an attitude. For a few days, they were no longer ruffled by the everyday events of life. It was as if they felt assured of their future, or perhaps didn't even care. They lived in the moment, and were, for that day or two, untouchable. Then they lived for a short while in the past, reliving their holidays, going on and on about how great it was until it became just a place they had been, somewhere to brag about.

When they went somewhere with the same climate as the UK or colder, Penny to New York in March for example, there was no such change. It was just a place to brag about from the day they got back.

But when they went to warm places, there was a change in their auras from the day they returned and it is this that Ellie understands now, sitting under the trees with the sun on her face.

The seat of her t-shirt dress is covered with pine needles when she stands, bringing with them the fragrance of the deeper layers, musky and rich. It feels like a long time since breakfast and she realises she is hungry. She has normally had about three milky coffees by now and wandered around for a pastry from the patisserie, the nearest one, by the travel agent's, on the other side of the railway station in the next village.

'Ha! Patisserie,' Ellie scoffs aloud. There is never any smell of freshly baked bread from that national chain 'patisserie' shop. Hot pizza slices, maybe. And all the biscuits are pre-packed. They do sell a good cream slice, though. That's her Friday treat—about as exciting as the weekends get these days. It seems sad for a nineteen year old. Maybe she will be able to get a cream slice here, but then she probably won't be bothered about it by Friday?

She walks a few steps with her head back to face the sunshine, eyes half-closed, only peeping to check where she is going to make sure she doesn't fall. She stops. A lizard slithers through the dried grass, pausing motionless on a stone to her left, before scuttering away. She continues when it has gone.

Going down the hill is so much faster than it was on the way up. She notices letters sticking out of the drawer-front letter box, and another lizard, smaller, brown, sits on the brass handle on top, basking in the sun. Down in the square, the bakery door is closed. The pharmacy, too, is lifeless. The *kafeneio* is shut. Her shoulders are burning hot now, and it seems best to go back for a late lunch and to see if she can buy some sun cream. They are bound to have a shop in the hotel.

Heading out of the bright village and walking along the lane towards the beach path, she is surprised to see Sarah sitting under an olive tree surrounded by goats. The surprise isn't that Sarah is there, but rather that she, Ellie, is here to witness such a sight. She would never have thought in a million years that she would have found a way to make this, her being here, happen. The brown, white, and black patches on the goats merge one into the other and it is hard to tell how many there are. Horns bob into vision, curling and gnarled, as the animals lift their heads to see who approaches. One look and the horns dip back to the ground, white stubby tails lifted, showing undersides of white, as they continue to graze. The dapple of their coats blends into the mottled shade under the tree. Some of them strain their necks up to reach the silver-blue leaves on the shorter olive trees. One has its front hooves halfway up a trunk, stretching to nibble on the lower branches.

'Hi,' Sarah calls to her.

'Hi, these yours?' Ellie asks. What a dumb thing to say. She grimaces.

'Yes, well no. Well yes,' Sarah says cryptically. It makes them both smile and relieves Ellie of her self-criticism. Sarah's streak of red lipstick is at odds somehow with her job, her cream dress, the caramel of the burnt earth and the soft, dark cyans of the olive leaves.

'Well I'm glad I asked.' She is relaxed with Sarah, as if she has known her for years. She must be

117

even older than Marcus. But she is not like a mum, not mousey and quiet. She is just, well, dignified, cool.

'Ah, it's a bit of a long story,' Sarah says. 'They belong to someone else. He left to rejoin his wife. But …'

Ellie does not want to intrude, but Sarah looks so comfortable sitting on her olive root in the shade that she steps closer, under the tree. Besides, Ellie is sure she can recognise a hint of a scandal in the words Sarah has spoken. Since her and Marcus' affair, she feels drawn to disparagements, with the need to compare maybe, to diminish her own. She sits.

'So they belong to someone else then.' Her invitation to talk sounds awkward to her own ears, but it is the best way she can think to say it.

'I suppose strictly they do. But as things are working out, maybe they won't.'

Ellie waits, not sure how to encourage her to say more. After watching the goats and wondering if she should go, she asks, 'Have you been here, in this country, long?'

'Long enough to fall in love.' Sarah laughs gently. 'He is the man whose sheep and goats these are. But he had a wife in Australia.'

'Oh, difficult.' Ellie likes that. At least Marcus didn't have a wife. That would have made an even worse scandal. Sarah picks up a small pebble and throws it at the feet of the nearest goat, which jumps

118

sideways and moves away, the rest of the herd following.

'He went back to try and patch things up.' Sarah sighs. 'But, it seems, that is not working out, so he is coming back.' With this, she looks straight in Ellie's face with an open smile, her eyes alive.

'Oh, how wonderful for you.' There is a little prick of envy at the love she can see reflected in Sarah's eyes. She thought she had that with Marcus in the first few days, but it dwindled so fast that it left her wondering if it was only she who was besotted, or even if she had just been caught up in the excitement of the events and it was nothing to do with him at all. The physical, intimate side of things petered out so quickly. In fact, there was never a repetition of what happened in the store cupboard, certainly never with that passion again.

'Can I ask you something? I don't mean to get all heavy, I'm just curious. You know that side of love that is all mystical and consuming? How long does it last?' With the sun kissing their skin and the warmth loosening their limbs, it does not seem such an inappropriate question. She cannot imagine ever asking such a question, say, at a wet bus stop in her hometown to someone she has only met a couple of times, but here, everything seems acceptable. Although it does make her sound a bit naïve, as if she has never loved, which, thinking about it, is true if you didn't count Marcus.

Besides, how else are you supposed to know these things if you don't ask?

'Why would it stop?' Sarah asks. 'Love is all that and more. You find the right person and that feeling can last forever.' She is silent for a second, and judging by her face, she is scanning through private thoughts. 'I have a Greek friend here. She is an old, old lady but she still has that feeling for her husband and theirs was an arranged marriage when she was in her teens. She didn't love him then, but as time passed, the spark ignited and she still has that feeling even though he is dead now.' A sadness crosses her face before she forces a smile to say, 'Why, have you met someone?'

Ellie rounds her shoulders, drops her head. Technically, she is a married woman. She is not ready for another scandal. No doubt she looks too young to Sarah to be married. Her hands dangle between her knees, out of sight, so she slips off her wedding ring. It will not fit the third finger of her right hand so she puts it on her little finger. Looking down at it to see if it just looks silly there, she finds it looks good, trendy even.

'My guess, by your silence and your red cheeks, is that you have. Welcome to Greece! If you don't fall in love with the country, you will fall in love with the people. They should hang warnings as you come through passport control.' The goats have gathered around them again and Sarah takes another well-aimed shot with a small pebble. They skitter away.

'You know, I'm going to miss you when you go back,' Sarah says.

Ellie blinks, swallows. 'Really?' Her cheeks feel a little hot and she looks away, focusing on one of the goats. A smile plays around the corners of her mouth but she does not allow it to fully form.

'Yes.' Sarah leans her back against the tree trunk and closes her eyes. 'There are times when I just need to speak to someone of my own culture. When you learn a language, at the beginning, you miss all the subtleties, the nuances, the inferences. Even with Stella, I speak on such a straight level.' Her eyes close, she looks so comfortable.

'But there must be many English tourists who come to the hotel,' Ellie says, taking the opportunity to really look at Sarah's reposed face. Sarah's eyes open a fraction and she smirks.

'Not everyone suits everyone.' She says the words with a sigh. 'There are two other English women in the village though, but they are not always around. I just miss the day-to-day chat the English do. The subjects are different. The Greek women talk about what they have cooked, what they will be cooking, if they have been out for coffee.'

'I suppose you don't know these things until you live somewhere. But you seem happy enough.' Ellie speaks slowly.

'In the night, you know, the small hours when your head tells you nonsense and your heart believes it, I sometimes wonder if I have done the wrong thing.' Sarah pulls a twig out from the dried grass; it has an ant walking its length. She puts it down gently.

'My family is so far away. I cannot have in-depth conversations about, oh I don't know, philosophy, whatever, and I wonder if I have isolated myself too much.'

Ellie shifts uncomfortably.

'But when the morning comes, the sun shines through the window, the goats bleat, and I cannot wait for the day.'

Ellie smiles at the conclusion but weighs up what Sarah has said. It is bound to be the small things that are missed. What would she miss? It is hard to think of anything, sitting under this olive tree in the warmth. Home is isolating, anyway. The whole thing with the press has left a shadow that she seems to walk under, scared to do too much, scared to say too much, scared to get to know people in case they recognise her from the tabloids. She wouldn't miss any of that.

'I'm not sure there is much I would miss.'

'You might be surprised.'

Little Lotherton comes to Ellie's mind, where she and Marcus have moved to. It must be one of the smallest villages in Yorkshire. In fact, it's barely a village, with just a single track lane. It only exists there because there used to be running water. Halfway up on the left is a nineteenth century mill that once spun wool, its power coming from the stream at the back that is now diverted to a thirsty pig farm. The mill's cobbled courtyard, where wagons pulled by horses would have once pulled up to deliver fleeces to spin and to collect the fabrics to take into Bradford to sell, is now used by a farmer to park his tractors and ploughing machines. The mill is where he stores his hay.

The mill's presence gave rise to the squat stone-built, slate-roofed weaver's cottages with their rows of tall, solid, mullioned windows upstairs to let in enough light for the weavers to do their work. With those days long gone, they are of little value now, the village being so far from civilisation. The place attracts people looking for cheap rent and a place to hide away from the pace of city life.

Little Lotherton is so small, it is not serviced by a train and is not on a bus route. The nearest public transport goes as far as the larger village across the valley that is known locally, and no doubt with some irony, as Greater Lotherton, or, even more colloquially, as The Town.

Greater Lotherton is just off the main road in to Bradford, The City. The main street in Greater Lotherton, after dipping to the bottom of the valley where the railway runs, then climbs the other side, heading directly for the moors. A good ten minute stretch of the legs up this road is required to reach Little Lotherton's cobbled lane.

Both villages are somewhat lost in time, and there is little Ellie can imagine she would miss if she were never to return again. Besides, no matter where she is in England, the fact remains that she was, however briefly, in the National papers.

'There was a spot of bother back in my home town last year and there was all sorts of rubbish talked about me. People who didn't know me judging me, that sort of thing. It would be great to get away from all of that.'

'That sounds very uncomfortable,' Sarah says. 'I think with regard that sort of behaviour, people are the same the world over.'

'So when does your man come back?' Ellie asks, consciously changing the subject.

'Any day. He is just looking for a ticket he can afford.' Her excitement is apparent. 'Right, I'd better get this lot back. I don't normally graze them at this time, when it's so hot, but with the official opening of the hotel tonight, I won't get any time off later.'

Ellie stands before Sarah does.

'I'd best get back too. What time do they serve lunch until?' Ellie asks.

Sarah looks at her watch. 'You've time if you go through here.' She points behind her. 'Just follow where the olives end and the orange trees start, and it takes you right to the hotel. It will also save you from burning if you stay in their shade.' She looks at Ellie's shoulders.' You need to get some cream on.'

Ellie takes her leave into the olive grove and looks back once to see Sarah refreshing her lipstick.

The olive leaves are a green-blue on one side, with a silvery sheen to them on the reverse. The slightest of breezes, smelling of salt and sea, drifts through, rattling them and making them flutter, showing first one side then the other. In comparison, their twisted trunks are dark. Studying them as she walks, she decides that one or two of them at least have started as many thin trunks that have grown and twisted together with age, creating holes and knots that she has never seen in other tree trunks. Everything seems magical in the warmth.

But she hasn't fallen in love. She has only seen him for seconds. She knows nothing about him. It's just that she can relate, with him being only a couple of years older than her, maybe. His age also makes a change from Marcus, not that she wishes a change exactly, just that she is a little tired of slippers by the fire, one drink at the Shepherd's Arms on a Saturday tea time, and all that time he spends with Brian, who, in her opinion, is just plain dull. But Brian teaches history at Marcus' new school, and it is probably good for Marcus to find a friend. She wishes she had. She knows no one where they live now.

Coming out from the shade of the trees, the sun chases away all negative thoughts. Her shoulders are truly burning now. She hurries across the lawn from the edge of the trees to reception.

The courtyard where she had breakfast is cool even in the heat of the day. All the umbrellas have been put up, one over each of the tables. What intimidated her this morning, the fear of being stared at, being alone, now is not even a memory. The same family that was there at breakfast is there again, one of the children sitting scowling, arms crossed. But the other diners are strangers. There is a couple sitting very close to one another drinking wine and an old man and woman eating whilst thumbing through a guide book and pointing at the pages. The old lady's hand is on the old man's leg.

Lunch is a cold buffet of local produce: ham and chicken, feta, yoghurt, boiled eggs, grapes, cheeses, and slices of amazing filo pastry pies.

After lunch, it is a toss-up between indulging herself in a short nap or going down to the beach, maybe having a drink.

The beach wins.

Going out of the front door to go round seems too long-winded, her patio doors mean stepping through flower beds so, instead, she heads deeper into the hotel. There is bound to be a second door at the side.

The corridor is silent, her steps muffled by the thick carpet and the air is conditioned and lifeless. A door marked *Emergency Exit* is not completely shut and it is going in the right direction. It opens onto a short, uncarpeted utility corridor with an open door at the far end, the path to the sea in sight.

Passing closed doors to her left and right, Ellie hurries to the light. It doesn't exactly feel forbidden to be here, but it is clearly not intended for guests. Just as she reaches the way out, the door to her left opens and Loukas steps out, carrying a crate of beer bottles. He looks up and his jaw drops open. The expanding of his pupils cannot be mistaken. She freezes on the spot. He puts down the crate.

'Oh I am sorry,' Ellie stammers, now quite sure that she should not be here. Loukas reaches out his hand as if to touch her face, but retracts it again. She steps towards the open door, leans to push it wider open for her. Her arm touches his chest. She is on him. Nose in his neck, lips on his skin, rising to meet his mouth. Hugging him tight so they touch in every possible place. She wants to consume him. Drink in everything that is not Marcus. Absorb his youth so it brings hers back to the surface, possess every inch of his tanned, smooth skin to coat herself with his beauty, soak in his dignity, his charm, his cool, and wear it like a trophy to show that it is not only the Penny Craigs and the Rebecca Slaters of this world that can be part of such gorgeousness. Her breath comes fast; she is lost to the moment.

Loukas cannot help himself. She is alive. His hands explore the curve of her waist, the arch of her back. Through the t-shirt dress, he can feel dimples, one either side of her spine at the base. She is moving faster than he is, her hands grabbing, hysterical, demanding. He cannot give her back what she is asking fast enough. Her lips are on his ears, warmer than the air; he cannot catch his breath. Every part of him is responding. If he lets this continue, he will be lost and he will take her with him, absorbing her, possessing her. For the briefest of seconds, he imagines them in the aftermath, exhausted, sweating on the floor amongst empty beer crates and rat traps. He grabs both her arms and pins them to her side in a bear hug. She struggles just once and then stops abruptly and looks into his eyes. He can see the fear of rejection ready to play its role. He won't allow that.

Slowly, very slowly, he moves his mouth towards her. When she rushes to meet him, he pulls back and begins again until she waits for him. The kiss is all and more than he expected. She is calm now. She, too, is immersed in the kiss and he is transported, out of his life, out of his loneliness that until this moment he had not recognised. Out of reality, they soar and sail in the endless blues of the Mediterranean sky and until they naturally part— mostly to breathe.

He is happy to just look now. Look into her eyes, see if everything he is feeling is returned. It is all there: the willing, the wishing, the promising, and the possibilities as she smiles.

'Loukas?' It is Stella's voice coming from somewhere outside. They jerk apart. Ellie blushes.

Loukas picks up the crate of beer, '*Edo*,' he calls and, with a last look back at her and a smile that chisels out the dimple in his cheek, he is gone.

'Oh my God, what am I doing?' Ellie's heart is beating so strongly, she can feel it in her ears, against her ribs, and her hands are shaking as she leans against the wall and relives some of the moments that have just passed. Marcus tries to invade her thoughts, soaking her emotions in guilt, trying to

128

drown her in remorse, but she pushes him to one side. At least it is not a storage cupboard in the art room of a secondary school in a cold and grey country. She mocks herself with her congratulations of going up in the world. But she knows her humour is a celebration—and a condemnation—of the wonderful thing that just happened.

Her liberation brings previously undreamt of thoughts. The first stings her sense of decency. To hell with Marcus and the marriage, a darker side of her wants to shout. The whole thing was all for his benefit anyway, to stop him being sacked. But he was sacked after all, so what was the point? To save face? They have no face in the one-street village they are in now. To stop the scandal about the baby? Well, there was no baby.

It is a dry laugh that escapes her. Her father will probably never speak to her again if she divorces. 'What will my congregation say?' He will cry. Well, sod him. Ellie pushes the outside door open with such force it swings back and bangs against the wall.

Stella is organising the beach bar with him. He cannot stop smiling. His cheeks are starting to ache.

'I didn't think working here would make you this happy,' Stella remarks. Loukas knows she is not a fool. He can hear the question. It occurs to him that he needs to be guarded, maybe not with Stella, but the village is small. Rumours of a casual fling with a tourist could have unbearable repercussions with the old man and old woman. But then maybe his future is not what it was? His stomach flips over at this thought. He decides to enter the conversation at an angle. She will understand.

'Your clients seem very pleasant.'

Stella glances at him, light in her eyes, a smile twitching at her lips, telling him that she has understood already. She plays along.

'Yes, the Internet is a marvellous tool. I am finding my feet marketing the hotel. It's not easy, but I am meeting some wonderful people, like the lovely girl, Ellie, who you met this morning.' Stella puts down the glass she is polishing and looks out to sea, her eyes creasing at the corners, uncharacteristically showing her age. 'But I sense that everything is not quite right for her. Maybe she is unhappy about something. She reminds me how I felt when I was trapped with Stavros.'

Loukas stops unloading the beer crates at the mention of Stella's first husband's name. He was a pig. But is Stella trying to tell him something more? He waits for her to continue.

'Someone so young should not be unhappy. If I had had children, I would have spent all my life making sure that they were not unhappy.' She continues to look out over the water, her face losing shape as her muscles sag.

Switching back to her normal self, she picks up another glass to polish and puts on a smile.

Loukas is sad that Stella never had children. He knows he is the right age to be her son and he knows that in some ways, he stands in their stead. Maybe Ellie is also filling a role for Stella in some way. Maybe that is some of the sadness she is talking about, something to do with Ellie's parents, perhaps, or maybe it is all her own sadness reflected.

Stella's situation is regrettable perhaps, but by helping others, she does all she can to help herself. She wants no pity.

'So you like the look of her, yes?' There is something he cannot pin down in the way Stella says it. A caution? But the question brings a heat from his neck, rising to his cheeks, so he continues to take the beers from the crates and put them in the fridge.

'What do you know about her?' He avoids directly answering her question.

'Nothing really. We exchanged a few emails. I am just guessing, really.' Stella is vague, but it is her discretion he counts on, too, so he has no objections.

'She did mention that she moved to a new town about a year ago and maybe that makes her lonely.' Stella has finished polishing the glasses and she wipes the bar top although it is already polished and clean. She looks him in the eye. It feels like a warning and he wonders what it is that she does not tell him. Is she worried about the old woman and old man's reactions if he becomes entangled? Is it about him or about Ellie or herself? Something is not clear.

Loukas nods. He knows Stella well enough to know that if she has not said something, she will not be induced to say it. If he wants to find any more about Ellie, he must ask her himself.

Ellie is bound to come down to the beach later. Linger at the bar. Sit with him a while.

He can find out all about her then.

Chapter 12

The door bangs back against the wall and swings closed again.

Ellie has not moved. She shivers in the air conditioning. It was fantastic, it was wonderful, it was all she ever dreamed it could be and it was completely out of order!

Does she never learn? What is she planning to do? Jump from one store cupboard to the next and each time give no thought to the consequences, using other people as a quick fix to improve her life? As the thoughts come, they dry her mouth and bring moisture to her eyes. The bright sunlight streaming through the door equals her epiphany, but clashes with her sorrow.

It is her feeling about his decency, his openness, his sense of responsibility, as well as his looks, that draws her to him. They are the things she is craving. The clean wholesomeness of him. But she cannot grab those in a store cupboard and expect them to survive, let alone put them on as an overcoat to hide all she is not.

The whispers at school ring once again in her ears. Words like 'tramp' and 'dirty' and 'whore.' Her lungs deflate and her head drops. She has just proved them right. Her next breath comes as a sharp intake that snorts its way into a sob. Turning on her heels, she runs to her room, fighting with the lock, almost pulling the curtains from the rail in her desperation to shut out the world, and then she throws herself face down onto the bed.

It's not fair. Marcus took away her innocence and her honour and made her embarrassed to face the world. Now his existence denies her something that seems so right, so natural.

No, that too is not fair. She cannot blame it all on Marcus. She played her part in the cupboard too, eventually.

But Becky and Penny made it seem so innocent, a joke, all part of growing up.

'Ohhhh.' She groans and curls into a ball. She has made such a mess of her life. She isn't someone who jumps from one man to the other, she just isn't. Yet events suggest otherwise. Why did she marry Marcus? Crazy, crazy, stupid! To shut her parents up? To shut the school up? Or in hopes for more passion, more of the stock cupboard?

She groans again. It's so childish. So ridiculously childish. She should have just pointed the finger at Marcus and if there had been a baby, she could have just dealt with it.

No she couldn't. She couldn't have done that. She could not have harmed an unborn child. No way.

But there wasn't a baby, so why didn't she get the marriage annulled when her period came? It seems so easy now to think like this. But at the time, everything seemed hard, the world against her, the school, her parents, the other kids. She was seeking a safe harbour.

Her breathing is laboured, the tightness in her chest gripping her heart. What if she just never goes back? Stay here, learn the language, get a job and… and what?

Unrealistic. As always, she is being unrealistic. Time to start thinking things through. Face her life. Be more responsible.

But hasn't that always been the problem, making decisions? What if she gets it wrong again? That's the fear! All that stuff Father lectures her about; morality, responsibility, consideration, the bands of his words squeezing tighter and tighter as she has got older until she couldn't move, couldn't make a decision that would fit all his regulations. So many of them seemed to condemn her, restrict who she felt she was, deny her feelings. Her interests in boys suffocated when she mentioned someone she quite liked at church nearly three years ago now. It seemed the topic was raised at the dinner table nearly every evening since. Mum quietly chaperoned her at church, ensuring that she stayed away from him and guilt made her stay away from any other boys she got on with, too. Stayed away and became the odd one out at school. Stayed away and became lonely. Stayed away until she found a man, not a boy. Then she made her escape. Her escape from the freedom to get it wrong by passing all the decisions to that man in one fantastic, passionate submission.

From then on, she was no longer responsible for the consequences; all the adults' eyes turned on Marcus. How much easier it is to give over that responsibility to someone else, anyone else, even Marcus.

She wants it back now. That right to choose. Isn't that why she is here? Isn't taking this holiday showing Marcus she has her own mind, her own choices, making a stand? Forcing herself to grow up, perhaps?

The tension around her chest releases its steely grasp a little. Thoughts of being responsible, growing up, seem to offer her some relief.

Rolling to sit up, she finds that the dressing table mirror is at the wrong angle and she can see herself: one of the straps of her dress off her shoulder, her lank hair, her eye makeup running. She looks like a tramp.

But what does she need to do to be grown up? The task appears Herculean.

Father's moral codes are all she has ever been offered as a guide to how to be responsible. Where do those fit here? She is married. That is a fact. To cast that aside is not responsible. She took a vow. There is not only her, there is Marcus. He took the vow too.

But they have so little together now. On the other hand, what about the old woman Sarah talked about? She had an arranged marriage and real love grew. Perhaps her impatience with Marcus is childish, too? Why does no one tell you about these things, how they go, what is normal?

Ellie kicks off her sandals and her feet slap against the tiled floor into the bathroom where she blows her nose and washes her face. Yesterday's knickers lay by the bath. She ignores them but then turns around and picks them up, finds a plastic bag amongst her things and starts a laundry bag. There! How grown up is that!

But she couldn't feel sadder. Nor can she stop thinking about Loukas.

'Okay.' She addresses the dressing table mirror as she sits on the bed. 'What happened? A quick kiss and a hug with Loukas, no big deal. It happens. Get over it. Have your holiday. Go home. Work on your marriage. Have some dignity. You are not a tramp.'

There, it is said. She has been told.

The words alone exhaust her. The request is too big; she is so small. She feels drained with it all. Curling up on the bed, she drifts with the heat until she is asleep.

Loukas puts a towel someone has left behind on the sun bed nearest to the bar, claiming it. Ellie can lay there, keep him company. It is a shame he has to work tonight of all nights, but he must. Stella is relying on him now; she cannot be let down again. Tomorrow maybe he can take Ellie out. Go to Saros town nearby and drink coffee in the square, talk, get to know her more. If any villagers see him, well too bad. He cannot stay single the rest of his life.

There's that guilt again. It comes every time he thinks of doing something that pulls him away from Natasha. But why? Even on her death bed, she made him promise to have a life, find a new love. So why the guilt?

Normally this question goes round and round unanswered, and today he does not expect it to be any different.

He takes the empty crate back to the stockroom, part of him hoping Ellie is still there. Even though the corridor and store room are empty, the feelings of being with her return and with them come some sort of answer. He didn't marry Natasha, lovely as she was, because he loved her. He married her wishing. Wishing she was someone else, someone like Ellie.

Even this thought stops him in his tracks. A slow exhale releases his disappointment with himself.

His first wish came when Natasha kissed him. He wished it would be electric, uplifting, soul expanding, that his world would move, like it just did with Ellie. But it didn't. It was sweet and kind and warm and comforting. Her tenderness like a kitten; his rejection would have been like a truck tyre. So they dated for a couple of months. Then they were invited, as a couple, to a university friend's engagement party, and that ignited the second wish.

His friend raved about how wonderful life was to be engaged. He ranted nonstop until Loukas began to think there was something he was missing. Did the fireworks and dazzle come with commitment? Was that what was needed? He considered and pondered. Then one night when he was half drunk, he proposed. The next day, in the sober light, she linked his arm and took him to a jewellers and he put a ring on her finger. Then he waited for his wish to come true. But there were no fireworks, no storm, nothing but blandness.

That is not to say it wasn't good between them. It was. It was good and decent and they did love each other. She would say so and he would nod in agreement. At one point, though, he had tried to call it off and he had almost got there, said the words that would have broken her heart but the auditorium filled with noise and the lecture began. By the time the lecture was over, he had lost his nerve and could not repeat himself. He never tried again, too much of a coward to bear the look that would have distorted her face. The look that said she knew she was about to be rejected and hinted at all the pain that would follow. He could see the anguish forming deep inside her and he lost his nerve and settled for cosy.

When they married, he hoped, wished, that their wedding night would bring what he desired. She was so keen and he went through all the motions, but if the temperature is not hot enough, the water will not boil. He tried, eyes open, tender kisses, eyes closed, concentrating on the physical and that is

140

what it became. All physical. Which was alright; it's better than a loveless marriage, but he still yearned for fireworks and rockets.

She could feel it. He knew she could. She wanted to make him happy, give him his fireworks. That was why, when she had nothing left to give, she made him promise to find someone else after she was gone. Her last desire was that he should have fireworks from her even if someone else stood, or rather laid, in her stead.

So there was his guilt. He cheated her. Cheated her short life of real love, real intimacy, and it seems wrong to move forward with his own happiness now. Was he trying to pay off his guilt by slaving for her mama and baba?

He cannot find any more crates of bottled lager. He is bound to run out tonight, with the whole village and most of Saros buzzing with the idea of the party. Sadness is consuming him.

He turns to leave, hoping again that Ellie will be just outside the door to lift him from all he is feeling, but there is nothing but a fly hurtling itself against the window above the door, the sunlight calling to it, forcing its actions in futile repetition.

He could hurtle himself into the light, too. He could throw himself at Ellie. Bounce against the outrage of his in-laws, rebound from the gossip of the village. He could. It would be easy. But it would not be kind or decent. Ellie promises everything, he can feel it, see it in her eyes. There is no need to hurry. Take it slowly, get to know her, be friends first, that is the foundation. Be respectful. She deserves that. The rest is there for sure.

Pulling at a folded tarpaulin just inside the storeroom door, he finds ten crates of beer neatly stacked. He'll take two and leave them behind the bar. The rest can stay here for now. At least he now knows where they are.

Outside, the heat is at its height for the day. The bar, with its palm-leaf roof, has an electric fan, but it just ruffles the hot air. There are only a few people on the sunbeds and, all except one who is going lobster red, have their umbrellas up. A mother covers her child in sun cream, the child standing stiff, arms out, trying to be helpful.

Ellie will come soon. She can sit at the counter, too.

He takes a tea towel from behind the bar and puts it on the stool nearest the half door that swings in and out of his new world, claiming that seat for her.

His excitement is growing. A new future is beginning to form inside his head. Maybe even a future in England, or maybe here at the hotel, Ellie by his side. There are no limits. The possibilities are endless. They can do anything.

Chapter 13

People have started gathering for the official opening, but Ellie is nowhere to be seen. A Greek woman in a purple dress, the highest of heels, and her hair piled on top of her head wriggles onto the end stool. His carefully placed tea towel falls to the floor.

Tables with starched white cloths have been distributed all across the lawns and the forecourt of the hotel. The opening speeches will be made in the foyer and then the guests will find their seats for the buffet-style dinner.

The cicadas are still singing in the orchards, confirming that the heat is not lessening with the onset of evening. As the sky fades from blue to orange, the ground-level lighting along the path edges is switched on. The hotel's car park is full, and new arrivals are obliged to park in the olive groves off the lane from the main road. The old man and old woman will turn up at some point to show willing, be neighbourly. It might be better for relations but part of him wishes, hopes, that they will not come, although he knows they will. 'Hypocrites,' he silently labels them. What a shock they will get when they see him behind the bar.

'No need to be unkind,' Loukas reprimands himself. He will explain to them that it is just one night, suggest that they get up to do the bread tomorrow. After all, just a year ago, they had done it every day all their working lives, boy to man for Natasha's baba. It will help them to move on, he will suggest. And if they do get up and make the bread for one day, maybe more will follow. He twitches his shoulders in excitement. He can almost feel the shackles releasing.

But where is she? It has been hours. Why did she not come straightaway? Mind you, he couldn't have given her any attention, he has had so much to do. No, it is better to see her when things calm down. That is probably what she is thinking, too, wait until after the opening ceremony.

More and more people are arriving. Someone is testing the sound system. '*Ena dyo, ena dyo, ena, ena dyo.*' The cooking smells grow stronger: onions, tomatoes, oregano, and roasting meat. The priest has arrived in his oversized shiny black four wheel drive. He lumbers from the backseat and it is just possible, through the crowds that are gathering, to see Stella greet him. The people close in around the man's black robes and tall black hat until Loukas can only see the backs of heads. He is being kept too busy with the drink orders from those who are now perched on stools around him. The sunbeds are empty of bathers. Instead, they have men in suits and women in their finest dresses sitting neatly on their edges, the women ensuring their heels remain on the wooden walkway that runs between the seats, the men pushing cigarette ends into the sand.

There is a hush around the hotel entrance. Everyone turns their attention in that direction. Then the drone of the priest comes over the speakers as he blesses the hotel, blesses the workers, blesses Stella, and blesses the crowd. He dips his rosemary branch in a bowl of holy water and, with a flicking motion, anoints everyone and everything he passes. As he walks, the crowds part and follow him between the tables and down to the sun chairs, all of which get a good sprinkle of water and some sacred words. Loukas and all the people on the barstools cross themselves three times, some lifting golden crucifixes on chains from their breastbones to kiss, all thanking the priest as water liberally speckles silk blouses and wets lacquered hair. The children's swings on the lawn are blessed, the roundabout, the swimming pool, even some of the balconies of the rooms.

There she is! Sitting on her balcony. Why there? Why not here? As the priest passes her, she is anointed too and she brushes off the droplets from her dress. She does not cross herself. Once the priest has moved on, Stella speaks to her and she gets up, goes into her room. No doubt coming around to be with Stella. That is Stella's way. She will include as many people as she can. The crowd reconvenes outside the foyer and a microphone whines and squeaks.

For about twenty minutes after the priest has completed his duties, Loukas is very busy. He forgets some of the cocktails he used to know and so he adds a twist in their name. He serves a Stella's Singapore Sling and a Mitsos Mai Tai, explaining that Stella's opening a hotel near the village makes everything different, including the drinks. A local electrician agrees with him, no doubt hoping the hotel will bring more work. The mechanic from the village, the one who built the dough mixing machine, talks about getting a loan to buy a car or two to start a rental business for the guests of the hotel; a carpenter says he has started to make bowls out of olive wood which Stella displays in a cabinet in the foyer, and he has sold three already. A girl whom Loukas recognises says she does all her friends' nails and she is in talks with Stella to convert a storage room in the hotel into a salon where she can offer treatments and facials.

The energy is high. The village is moving with the times. The cocktail orders flow fast and it takes up his time mixing them. He could do with some help. When business calms for a few minutes, he mixes up three jugs of a cocktail he invented when he worked in a bar in Athens. Back then, he called it the *Meleti Meli*, the Honey Study. He told students it made their studies sweet and sold buckets of it every night. Now he takes a pen and writes out a sign with a new name. '*Tyxi tis Tsiganas*' -'Luck of the Gypsy'.

Within the hour, all three jugs are empty, sold out. They all want to toast Stella, share a bit of her luck.

'Hasn't she done well?'

'She has worked so hard!'

'I could do with her luck!'

He mixes another batch. Looking up to see who to serve next, he swallows hard when he notices the old man and old woman are hovering to his right, their faces set in stone.

The old woman opens her mouth and steps forward to speak to him.

Loukas leans as far as he can over the bar top to speak into her ear.

'Whatever your views, do not spoil this night for the hotel. This,' he indicates all the people around him, 'can only be good for the village.' He slides back to his side and stares at her, daring her. He can see the indecision on her face but eventually her features soften slightly.

'A glass of orange juice,' she says.

'I think I'll try a glass of the Gypsy's Luck,' the old man states and the old woman narrows her eyes and looks sideways at him. Loukas does not charge them. They remain near the bar as the opening speeches conclude and the Mayor of Saros steps up to cut the ribbon. The area around the bar thins of people and the old man moves nearer.

'I think you will be tired to get up tomorrow.'

'As you always are.' Loukas emphasises the word 'always' and instantly regrets it. He didn't mean to be so harsh. There's that look, that frail old man weakness in his eyes. Loukas hesitates as he thinks how to phrase what he really wants to say.

'You know, old man, sometimes we find our strengths by doing the things that feel the hardest.' He smiles and makes eye contact so as not to appear threatening. He leans towards him. 'Maybe if you decide to get up tomorrow,' he wants to say 'to become a working man again,' but that also sounds like a judgement so he quickly rephrases, 'to do what you have always done best, you might find the very action fills you with the zest for life you have always had.' He finishes his speech with a light touch to the old man's hand, the one that is gripped around his glass of Gypsy's Luck.

The aged look of frailty lingers in his father-in-law's eyes for a moment, watery and pale irises, then, almost imperceptibly his chin shifts down and to the side and his eyes half close and up again. The Greek 'yes' without the need for words.

'Another glass?' Loukas asks gently, but the old man puts his hand over his glass, implying he has to get up in the morning. Loukas' stomach turns. He cannot help but keep glancing into the crowd, looking for her. He has so much to say. The speeches have come to an end and there is a surge toward the buffet tables inside. All the people around his bar drift away; even the old man and old woman in their Sunday best melt away into the sea of sequins and sharp suits.

Now would be a good time for Ellie to come and be by his side.

The diners, balancing full plates, find their seats. Stella is at the top table with a selection of important guests. Mitsos is by her side, naturally, and there's Ellie on her other side, looking a little confused and lost. At the same table are the mayor, the priest, Babis the lawyer, and some people from Saros town council. All talking loudly, pouring from one of the five wine bottles he put on each table earlier.

This might be a good moment to fetch some more crates of beer and get rid of the empties. He takes two empty crates inside and returns, straining with the weight of two full ones.

'Ah, there you are.' Stella is by the bar with a plate of food in her hand. 'This is for you, are you hungry? Have you been busy?'

'Everyone is having a good time. I congratulate you, Stella.'

'That is in their nature. Save your congratulations for when we have another party a year from now because we are still up and running.' Her smile makes all her words light; her eyes are shining. She looks so alive. Her usual sleeveless floral dress has been exchanged for a grey lace shift and Loukas has never seen her look more beautiful.

'I wish you ease in its running, loyalty in your staff, and pleasant guests to stay.' Loukas takes a glass from behind the bar. 'Here, have a little of your own luck.' He points to the sign by the jugs, which

150

she reads and laughs. 'I have sold nearly six jugs of the stuff.'

'Well, long may my own luck continue then,' Stella responds, exchanging plate for glass. 'I have picked a creative thinker to run my bar!' She takes a sip and nods her appreciation.

'This looks good. Thank you.' Loukas picks up the fork. 'How is Ellie coping over there?' He must know why she has not come over.

'She seems a little distracted, actually. I will talk to her if I have a moment. She is young, I think, for her age. Maybe she wasn't ready for this holiday.' Loukas has seen the mothering look on Stella's face before but he is more interested in knowing what she means by her last comment.

'Not ready?' he repeats, hoping she will say more.

She waves at Mitsos, who is standing, looking over peoples' heads by the hotel's front doors, seeming a bit lost. She continues to wave until Mitsos sees her and gives a little wave back.

'I'd better go. I'll see you later.' Stella lifts her glass to Loukas as she leaves.

It is quiet after she has gone. He can even hear the lapping of the waves. The murmurs of the diners' voices blow away from him, inland, by the slight sea breeze.

Having eaten his plate of food, he sits back on his stool as the bouzouki player takes up a tune. The musician plays whilst the guests eat dessert, but some of the women cannot resist and one by one, they stand and gather to dance. The melodies pick up and the more lithe men join them. Loukas watches from afar. A part of him would like to be in there dancing with the rest of them, a guest, but he is also content to be sitting in the evening without the pressure of watching the time, thinking he should be in bed.

A lone figure breaks from the group. He recognises her outline. But she heads away from the bar to the end sunbed, where she sits. Why there? Why so far away? Is she playing games, teasing?

Fine, he can play games too. This is as good a time as any to collect some of the used glasses. Taking a tray, he gathers the ones nearest to him first, not looking at her. If she is staying away for a reason, he does not want to appear pushy. God forbid that she has changed her mind. Maybe he was mistaken and the kiss was not for her as it was for him. He glances at her. No, she felt the same way, he is sure. Her eyes said so much. He calms his racing heart and, when he is within earshot, he asks casually, 'Are you having a good time?'

'Oh, Loukas. Yes fine. Thank you.' Cold, distant.

'Everything alright?' His heart is out of his control. She must be able to see it thumping through his shirt.

'Yes, why wouldn't it be?'

There is definitely something wrong. He puts his tray down.

'Hey, what is it?' He sits beside her, his arm casually, tenderly around her shoulder. She shrugs it off.

'Nothing.'

She cannot look at him. Would she see hurt in his eyes? But better to hurt now than pretend everything is alright, grow increasingly fond of him only to leave for England in two weeks and never see him again. How cruel would that be? To both of them.

'Ellie?'

Even the sound of his voice hurts, tears at her insides, the knowledge that what she desires will never be.

'Ellie? Am I mistaken? Is what I thought, what I hoped, not?'

She cannot speak. If she makes any sound, she will either cry or give in. She should have stayed with the crowd, she should have gone onto the lane for some space, not here.

'I thought we both knew.' Loukas has a break in his voice. He sounds so young.

Trying to swallow, she takes in air. It sticks like a lump in her throat, so painful.

'I think I must have been wrong. I think I must have imagined something that was not. When I looked into your eyes, I saw such possibilities, I saw my dreams. If I am wrong, you must tell me.' The break in his voice is stronger now. If she looks at him, she knows she will see tears in his eyes.

'Please Loukas. It is not that easy,' is all she manages.

'Of course. All life is not easy, and all life is easy. It depends on your focus.' He reaches out and takes her shoulders, turning her towards him.

'Focus here Ellie, and you will not be afraid. I will make you safe. Together, we make our worlds complete.'

She's going to cry. The tears are there. Pulling herself from his grasp, she stands and runs back to the crowd.

Loukas watches her go. She takes with him his hope. His freedom from the bakery, his children, his old age.

A man saunters to the bar and stands tapping on the counter to the timing of the music. 'Eh, he's good, no?' he calls cheerily to Loukas, his head nodding in time to the bouzouki.

Chapter 14

The stars are visible in their thousands, the black between showing pinpricks of even more distant stars if he stares for long enough. Galaxy after galaxy spinning away. This is the time he normally gets up to start making the bread. Tonight it's the time the last person staggers away from the hotel. Stella, linking arms with Mitsos, head held high, shoes in her hand, left hours ago with Loukas telling her not to worry, he would take care of the bar and clear the tables, which he has done. The night manager, who arrived early for the tail end of the party, drank beer and helped clear up. Now his bubbling, snuffling snores echo from behind the reception desk, his head back, mouth open, hands linked across his chest.

Loukas closes the foyer doors to stop stray dogs making the newly laid carpet their bed for the night.

Ellie avoided him all night. After that one conversation, he only saw her from a distance, recognisable by the youthful energy of her movements and the whiteness of her skin. His rib cage is tearing apart, the ache of his heart so physical it brings anger which he expresses as he carelessly heaves over to the back door of the kitchen the boxes of glasses and beer bottles which he has collected from the beach. He dumps them on the ground, walks away.

He was not mistaken about what they felt. Something must have happened. Tomorrow he will find her and they will talk. It will be alright. She is scared maybe, but so is he. How often does this sort of lightning strike?

The way to the village through the olive and orange groves is difficult at night when the moon is not full. But tonight, the pale globe hangs low and large and it is almost as day. He emerges by the church, its small blue neon cross above the tower glowing, colouring the tarmac. He trots down between ghostly cottages to the square, hopeful that the lights are on in the bakery, that the old man has got up to make the bread. With his breath held, he turns the corner. No lights. His shoulders drop; he sighs heavily. It was too much to hope. First Ellie and now the old man. It seems that two wishes is too much to ask. One would have been enough.

His tread slows, he thrusts his hands in his pockets and ambles the last few yards. Then he blinks, the sudden light blinding him. As his eyes adjust, his spirits lift. The light in the bakery has come on. The old man is up. With renewed vigour, Loukas jumps twice on the spot, fists clenched, hissing 'Yes, yes!' and without any further hesitation he turns and walks away. The old man is up. The old man can make the bread. One chain has been released. His breathing grows deep and easy. The stars about him shine more brightly.

His soft shoes are noiseless as he marches, climbing the lane up past Mitsos and Stella's house. The brass handle of the drawer front that is the roof of their homemade letter box shines in the moonlight. Their cottage, down the lane beyond the gate, is engulfed in darkness. He climbs higher, up to the trees that tuft the top of the hill. Sitting heavily, his last pocket of energy used up, exhaustion washes over him. He has been up and going since the very early hours of yesterday morning. Maybe with some sleep he will make sense of what has happened with Ellie.

He watches the light in the bakery for some minutes, imagines the process the old man is going through. His wiry frame will, so easily, take the weight of the work, just like it always had. The old man is not that old after all. He wonders if the old woman is up making her man a coffee.

Will there be a future when Ellie makes his coffee? Will he ever have the pleasure of making hers?

With this thought, he leans back into the soft pine needles. The sounds of tiny insects scuttle by his ears. The early morning drop in temperature is upon the village, but at this time of year, every day is hotter than the last. Now, the pre-dawn chill is only just perceptible, making the air comfortable rather than cold, but under the trees there is a dew, a dampness. The pine tops move slightly, whispering her name. The moon has a halo around it, showing him that the world is a magical place and anything can happen. He knows he is right about Ellie. He just needs to talk to her. He closes his eyes.

Morning comes but Ellie sleeps on. As she wakes, the heaviness in her chest makes her wish she was still sleeping. She lays still, convincing herself to be responsible, adult. By the time she dresses, the heaviness has not subsided and the weight of all she feels for Loukas and all she is denying herself remains. Breakfast will have been cleared away by now. But when she goes to explore, she finds it is still being served by sleepy-looking staff who yawn and rub their eyes.

Sarah is sitting at a table sipping coffee, and she smiles and points to a spare chair. As Ellie pulls it out and its legs grate against the gravel, Sarah grimaces.

'Sorry,' Ellie says and puts down her coffee. She dreamt about him. He is in her every thought. It is worse than yesterday. She needs some company to take her thoughts somewhere else, talk about her life back in England, make it real again.

'Hangover,' Sarah mutters in explanation, her head in her hands. 'Did you enjoy it last night?' she asks quietly, dropping something that fizzes in her glass of water. 'Did you dance?'

Ellie cannot find the enthusiasm to talk. So she shakes her head instead.

'I did. On the table, dancing, ouzo in hand. Shameless! I got a letter from him yesterday. He is coming at the weekend!' Sarah announces.

'Oh, I am so pleased for you,' Ellie says, her own concerns lost in the moment.

'Not as pleased as I am.' Sarah is looking up at the blue sky.

'Why is it that love never runs an easy course? My friend, the old lady who is still in love with her dead husband—who also, as it happens, is the mother of my man, Nicolaos.' She gives Ellie a sly sideways look and a smile, inviting her into the new details of her life, 'says, "It is the course that love runs that makes it strong." What do you think Ellie? You think a rough course will make love stronger or do you think a nice, smooth course lets it flow?' Sarah pours a cup of tea. For someone with a hangover, she is remarkably animated.

The young man who carries the guests' bags to their rooms and does other odd jobs around the hotel puts his head through the arch of the courtyard. 'Sarah, the people in room four say there is a bag missing.'

'It's behind the reception desk,' Sarah replies.

He backs out of the way as a plump lady dressed in white comes in with a fresh batch of toast. The smell permeates the air and several of the other diners stand and hasten over to collect it whilst it is hot.

The moment for Ellie to answer Sarah's question has passed, but it lingers in her thoughts.

She and Marcus have had a tough course, but it has not made their love grow strong. It stopped her really considering how she felt. But this turmoil with Loukas is something else. There is nothing in her mind except him. Maybe if she gave into him it would run its course within the week and her life would go back to normal.

'So where do you live in England?' Sarah asks.

'In the north, Yorkshire. I moved recently.' This is her chance to remember all she has back home, where her real life is, and exclude Loukas from her thoughts. 'To a really cute village. Just one street, high up on the moors. The people there are interesting.' She has not really made friends with anyone yet but she has gathered some information about who lives in some of the houses.

'Hm, sounds intriguing.' Sarah sips her tea.

'Nev—he's got long hair, thin guy, a builder with a Salvador Dali moustache and a narrow goatee beard lives in the top house with his wife who is so tiny, her twelve-year-old twins are taller than she is. The locals call them King Nev and Queen Helen, on three accounts.' Ellie is starting to enjoy herself. Sarah seems to brighten from her hangover, looking over her cup.

'The village is a street on a slight hill which bends left at the top, around the walled courtyard of the old mill the weavers' houses were built for. So the first reason they are King and Queen is their house is at the end of the village. The very last one at the top.'

Sarah pours Ellie more coffee, encouraging her to keep going.

'The second reason is because their house is bigger than all the rest. It's two houses; the one knocked through to the other at right angles to it. So now it is two rooms downstairs and two rooms upstairs. Although I've not been in, I've just been told about it. And the third reason is that Nev has a sense of personal style. He wears clothes that look as if he has walked out a Thomas Hardy book. You know, collarless shirts with rolled-up sleeves, wide, buckled belts that hold up rough serge trousers and boots that look like they have been reclaimed from some coal pit worker from Sheffield. I know that for myself, I see him going up the street to his home nearly every day.' Ellie looks at the remains of their breakfast. Sarah offers her the last slice of toast.

'Like I said, Queen Helen is tiny and pretty, with wavy dark hair that falls below her waist and everything about her says she is a queen of the fairies or elves. She is quite unreal as she is so small but so perfectly formed with relatively long legs and a nipped waist. I stood behind her once, waiting to be served in the Patisserie, and I couldn't help but just stare. You know how some people are, you just want to stare at them.' Ellie looks for confirmation from Sarah, who nods in agreement. She has settled back in her chair and seems to be content just listening and nursing her hangover.

'The house next to King Nev and Queen Helen along the top of the street is empty. And the next after that is rented to a smiling, pretty, plump girl with a ring through her nose, who says she is a white witch but apparently she is doing nothing with her life, just claiming benefits.' Ellie hears how this might sound like unkind gossip and so adds, 'This is information I got off the Italian woman who lives next door to us. The day we moved in, she offered me coffee and then told us about everyone who lives in the street. I couldn't stop her.'

'Maybe she was lonely,' Sarah offers.

'Maybe. It's the people who live in the top corner house where the road bends that I feel sorry for. An old couple who complain about the decline of the neighbourhood. It must be hard to be somewhere so long and then see it dramatically changing.'

Sarah nods again, her eyebrows rising. 'Well, it depends how it changes, I suppose. This hotel will change the village, bring more tourists, more work perhaps. Mostly people only see it as being a good thing. There are exceptions of course, but I think those people are just bitter.'

'Oh, let me tell you about the man the next house down, next to the old couple. I've only seen him from a distance but they call him Septic Cyril and if the wind is in the wrong direction, even we can smell his house and we are near the bottom of the street.' Ellie laughs but the memory screws up her nose.

'It sounds as if you will never get bored there,' Sarah says. Ellie thinks to tell her of the house below Cyril's, where a reformed Hell's Angel lives.

No one knows quite how he makes his money, and next to him is a woman who has too many children for her age. The rumour is that every time she has a problem that she cannot handle, she distracts herself by getting pregnant. She is on benefits, too, with social workers coming and going all day long. Her house is directly opposite the mill. Then there are houses on both sides of the cobbled road, and Ellie knows nothing about who lives in them. The Italian woman was keen to continue her monologue describing her fellow villagers, but by this time, Ellie's mind wandered, wondering where Marcus was putting things in the house as he unloaded boxes and bags from his car. Speaking about the village makes it feel very close now, as if she could walk there.

'The Italian lady, Angela, has offered me coffee since but so far, I haven't gone.' The woman seemed to be a bit of a busybody and maybe not the best person to team up with in such a small community, not before meeting some of the other neighbours. But that hasn't happened either, as most days she is off walking on the moors, exploring the rocky outcrops. That's good; she misses the moors. She should focus on that, make it grow stronger until she cannot wait to get back home.

'What are you doing today then?' Sarah asks.

'I think I might go down to the beach. Sunbathe and swim.'

'Good idea. I think I'll stand behind a desk for eight hours trying to be helpful.' Her mouth twitches into a smile and then she swallows the last of her fizzing water. 'Right, that's me. I'll see you.' And she is gone.

Ellie pretends to herself that she is not half-looking out for him as she goes down to the beach, but the bar is closed. She swims and sunbathes and eventually falls asleep. When she wakes, the bar is open, the towels off the pump handles, bottles on the bar top, and Loukas has his back to her, pouring a drink for a lady in a wide-brimmed hat. He is more tanned than she remembers.

Before he turns around, Ellie gathers up her things and slips back to the hotel, praising herself for being responsible and mature. She somehow got the impression that he was only working there for the night of the opening. If he has taken it as a permanent job, this could make the next two weeks awkward. Putting her things on her bed, she realises she has forgotten the sun cream she found by the sunbed. It was nice, it smelt of coconuts, but she is not going back to get it and risk another conversation with him. Her resolve is not that strong. She picks up a book that was in her room when she arrived. It is not the kind of thing she would normally read, but it will do. It is entitled *The Illegal Gardener* and has something to do with migrant workers.

The next day, she decides to avoid the beach, telling herself it is the right thing to do. It is the sort of advice Father would have given her. Catching the bus into Saros town is interesting. Only three old ladies get on with her, each wearing a black skirt, blouse and headscarf. The bus is high off the ground and Ellie looks down on the orange groves they pass. Small huts are dotted in amongst the trees and tall grey pylons support huge fans, one to each field. It is very alien to her eyes.

Once in Saros, she spends a couple of hours looking around the shops. They sell touristy things; handmade jewellery, key rings with olive wood carved fobs, and there are some very chic dress shops with prices to match, an ice cream parlour with a sign in Italian. In amongst these shops are cafés and tavernas, each colourfully and loudly filled, mostly with Greeks. Not Greeks like in the village and the hotel though; these Greeks have a different feel. Their hair is well cut and their clothes designer. Maybe they are from Athens, down for the weekend. In the main square, which is back from the harbour front, there are what look like mosques at either end, both at an odd angle to the square's geometry.

'Facing east,' Ellie mutters to herself and from some distant classroom lesson, she seems to recall that Greece was occupied by the Turks at some point in time. The mosques give the square real charm, and the smaller of the two has glass-fronted notice boards outside, advertising plays and music. It is now being used as a theatre. The other buildings edging the square are all cafés at ground level, with flats, presumably, above. Boys play football in the central open area and more than one young child is being pushed on a tricycle, and one is on a bike with stabilisers. Two teenagers, younger than Ellie, stand with skateboards in hand, posing as if about to do a trick. Ellie watches them for a few moments and soon recognises them as the type of boys that are all talk and no action. It seems strange that such behaviour is cross-cultural.

The café in the far corner of the square offers shade under a huge spreading and ancient-looking plane tree, and only one free table with two chairs.

'*Parakalo*?' the waiter asks her, pulling out a chair, inviting her to sit. She is thirsty. A drink would be good but she has no idea what he has said.

'I, er…'

'Ah, yes please?' He quickly swaps languages.

'Just a coffee please, oh no, a chocolate.' Ellie looks down the menu as she decides.

'*Zesto*, hot? Or *krio*, cold?' The waiter scans the other tables as he speaks, one hand on his money belt, the other holding a tray.

'*Krio*.' Ellie smiles.

'And a black coffee,' a voice from behind her calls out, and Loukas pulls out the chair next to her and sits.

For a moment, she has no words. He smiles and all the tension she has been holding in her neck and down her spine releases. She feels suddenly light.

'So, I want to know. What has happened?' He is nothing if not direct. 'You are scared, yes? Me too!' I can see you feel the same… We are scared because we know we have been hit by lightning, we are scared because we may be making decisions that will affect the rest of our lives, we are scared because we can see each other with grey hair and wrinkles. Of course we are scared. But it is not a fear to run from. It is something to be embraced. I have thought of nothing but you since we met. I can tell by the way you look at me now that you have thought of me. So we can play this game if you like: You can run, I can chase you, it will be fun, but the outcome is already decided, so is that how you really want to spend these first days?'

The waiter is too quick; he is back already. A syrupy cold chocolate with two coloured straws and a wooden swizzle stick with a top of metallic paper hair is set before her. It looks childish. Loukas' coffee comes in a small serious cup on a saucer and it reminds her that she must be like the coffee and not the chocolate: responsible, adult. Loukas takes a sip of his drink and regards her over the rim. As for words, she can find none. He looks up as if he has been waiting.

'Ellie, speak to me.' He leans towards her and takes her hands. She pulls them away, slowly, unwillingly. 'Why are you torturing yourself?' He moves his chair closer, strokes her hair, his brown eyes rich, his pupils dilated. Part of her, the part that was so hurt by Marcus' quick cooling, the part that was shocked by the school's stance towards her and by the papers' violating remarks wonders if she is being naïve again. It's possible. Her track record does not prove her to be a very good judge of these things. Maybe he says this to all the foreign girls. He smells of something vaguely sweet and musky. Some of the froth from his coffee is on his upper lip and before she can stop herself, she wipes it away with her thumb. He grabs her hand and kisses it, and a tremble begins somewhere deep inside of her, all her misgivings evaporating. Twisting her hand, she loosens his grasp, avoids his lips on her fingers, and takes a hold of her drink. It feels cold, wet. She needs to stay strong.

'Okay, we play.' He sits back.

'It's not a game.' The words come out as if she is cross, which she isn't.

'Then why?'

She could tell him, just say straight out that she is married. But somehow, despite the wedding and the certificate and the rented house they share, it does not feel true. It feels like a lie. She is not married with her heart and with Loukas, it feels really important to only speak from her heart. But it is her marriage that means they cannot be together, so she should tell him, explain. Maybe he can find a way round the problem.

But it is so few days before she returns home. Does she really want to spend that time telling this beautiful man the mistakes she has made, the loneliness of her life, the future she will have to live out in order to be adult and responsible for the consequences of her actions?

It is all so messy and ugly. Can she not keep this pure?

'We can be friends,' she says. 'I would deeply like to be your friend whilst I am here. Just enjoy each other's company, but don't ask me for more.'

'Tough. I do not ask for your friendship, I ask for all of you. I ask for your body, your mind, your soul, your temper, your love, and to kiss your chocolate mustachio.' And he leans forward and does just that.

Chapter 15

She did not pull away and she did not slap his face. Her lips remained soft and, even though the sensation was slight, he is sure they parted.

'Loukas…' She doesn't say any more but she shakes her head. Her eyebrows raise in the middle, a glistening on her lower eyelash. She may even be trembling.

'Tell me Ellie, *agapi mou*, tell me why you tremble.' He waits but no further words come from her. The café and square are so noisy. The women who sit drinking coffee around them shout their welcomes to those who join them. Several yiayias shriek commands at their grandchildren, causing him to wince. Even the boys playing football seem to be shouting louder than usual.' Do we need to go somewhere quiet? Would that help?' Loukas asks, but Ellie looks down and sadly shakes her head. 'How can I help?' He reaches for her hands but she draws them back. Looking up, she meets his gaze and she holds him there. The sounds recede, the smell of coffee and expensive perfumes are no longer recognised by his senses. There is only her.

'I am nineteen.' She says as if it were a crime.

Relief rushes over him and he smiles, begins to laugh. So big a deal about no problem at all! But there is no visible relief for her and his own tension returns, his laugh dies on his lips.

'Last year, I was still at school.' The tone of her voice implies there is more. Wiping all expression from his face, he leans forward to listen as closely as he can.

'There was a teacher.'

Telling him everything is the only natural and honest thing she can do, but it must be all the tale, not just the outcome. Explaining the taunting and teasing of Penny and Becky when they were meant to be her friends is easier than she imagined. Loukas moves his chair closer.

'So when Mr Cousins invited them into the stock cupboard and they excluded me, it hurt. I felt rejected. It felt like Sunday lunch.'

'Sunday lunch?' Loukas asks. Ellie gives a small sigh. Sunday lunch is going to be harder to talk about than Marcus.

'Sundays after my dad's service—he's a vicar—we had a big roast lunch. He was always so full of himself from preaching that he would continue it at the dinner table. Mum was up and down, in and out, carrying things to the table from the kitchen. I often thought she left things in the kitchen on purpose so she could get away when Dad started on one of his sermons. I would even offer to

173

help, but she would wave me away and Dad would tell me to sit down. Then he would begin.

'All my schoolmates would be out on a Sunday, hanging around, going shopping, at each other's houses, trying on makeup. I can see what they were doing now, finding themselves, deciding how they wanted to be in the world. A day of freedom whilst I sat at home. Dad's congregation of one. And as he talked, his eyes bore into me and his remarks became more and more personal, spitting about good and evil and the ways of the world, the loose morals of today's teenagers, the way the girls dress with their short skirts and crop tops. It felt like condemnation and rejection of everything I was, or could be.' Ellie tries to glance up to get some sort of reaction from Loukas but she cannot meet his eyes. Her cheeks feel like they are burning and she wants to stop talking but the words just keep coming out.

'Each statement he would enforce with a tangible example.'

It was normal. Normal as in it happened every Sunday and she cannot remember a time it did not happen. Maybe when she was very small, but she can remember it when her eighth birthday fell on a Sunday, so from way back. Mum witnessed it and said nothing, so it must have been normal. It was one of the things in life that just is and if she doesn't like it, then it is her making fuss. But now, speaking it out loud to Loukas, thinking about what happened, it seems far from normal.

174

'When he spoke of skirts being too short, if I had a skirt on, he would lean over and around the table leg and say 'Skirts up to here!' and he would push my skirt up and pull a face as if he was disgusted. No love, no thought, it was as if I, as a person, did not exist, or if I did, I was disgusting to him. If I had trousers on, his hand would run up my thigh to show me how high.' Ellie can remember the many times when the laundry had not been done and she had no trousers on a Sunday, so she would sneak into the utility room whilst Mum was cooking, pull out a dirty pair, wear winter tights underneath no matter how hot the day.

'And crop tops! He had this thing about crop tops.' Swallowing is not helping the words to come out and the cold chocolate looks thick and gooey. 'He would show me how high those were, too.' She can say no more, but the memory of the back of Father's hand pushing up under her breast, the edge of his little finger digging into her ribs to show her exactly how high. As she developed physically, she felt increasingly ugly. Her right to her own body violated, her breasts her enemies just for being there. Woolly jumpers did not help. She would grow hot, her face would grow red and sweat, and he would tell her to stop being so silly and take them off, refusing to carve the joint until she did so. The cabbage growing cold, a skin forming on the gravy. Then he would complain that the food was inedible and he would push it away until Mum got up and boiled fresh cabbage, the meat keeping warm in the

175

oven, and the whole procedure would start again. There was no winning.

'That is not right.' Loukas' words shock her. She looks up at him, feels a sense of hope but she is not sure what for. There is anger in his eyes. It is the first time she can recall someone siding with her, and it is very satisfying to see. No one has ever spoken a bad word against her saintly father before. 'But this was not your fault, *agapi mou*. This is something to recover from. But it does not change what we have. I will not be like your baba. I will be respectful.'

She could leave it there, holding onto the salvation he has offered from her father. He has forgotten what she was saying about Becky and Penny and Marcus, Mr Cousins. If she says no more, she can have an amazing two weeks.

'There's more.' Damn her honesty. His face says tell me, and that he will not judge her.

'Yes, your unkind friends and your teacher?' Loukas has not forgotten.

'Mr Cousins was not like the other teachers. He talked to us like we were people. He told us jokes and he made us feel like we were pretty, like we were women. Well, Penny almost was. She was the oldest in the year. I was the youngest, and it showed.'

'Tell me.'

'Well, Marcus, Mr Cousins, invited them into the stock cupboard and Becky pushed me back out, shutting the door behind them. There was giggling and talking, but all I could feel was that they had the same disgust in me as Father had shown. They found

176

me unacceptable as he found me and I stood outside that closed door for a couple of minutes until I ran to the toilets. I stayed in the last cubicle until after lunch.'

'That is very sad,' Loukas says.

She could still back out, still not tell him. At the moment, her tale is just sad. If she tells more, he will reject her just like Father, Becky, Penny, and Marcus.

Forcing herself to take a drink of the cold chocolate, the sounds of the crowds around her become noticeable again. She lifts her head up and throws her hair back. There. She has control; she is done. She will say no more.

'But there is more, yes?' His words pull her back down. The noise around her recedes again, her shoulders curl over, her head drops, her elbows rest on her knees. Loukas bows his own head and their hair touches. If she breathes regularly and focuses on the table leg, she will not cry.

'He invited me into the cupboard.' Loukas' fingers find hers. 'Because I felt excluded before, I agreed. But there was no Becky and no Penny with me. I was alone with him.'

Loukas' grip on her fingers tightens and then releases her to stroke her fingertips.

'Marcus, Mr Cousins, showed me some of the designs for pots he was working on. It felt personal, intimate. I felt special. We stood shoulder to shoulder as he turned his notebook pages, on the shelf with his own personal pottery tools, spatulas, old dentistry

177

tools in a box beside it. Then his hand was on my shoulder. Loosely, just resting. It crept up to my ear and his fingers played with my earlobe. I did not feel rejected. I felt as if he cared. Then his hand was on my leg, below my skirt hem, where Father would start with his sermon. I looked in his eyes, ready to face his rage, the rejection that I saw in my father when he did the same thing, but there was none. Then he pushed up my skirt. No sermon. It was like a release, an acceptance. His hand came away from my skirt and to my blouse. But it was not the back of his hand. It was the palm of his hand and it felt gentle. He kissed me lightly on the mouth.' Loukas' grip has grown tight again.

The kiss was like those she had seen at the cinema. She was not sure she liked it. His tongue too insistent, she thought she might choke. His hand rushed from blouse to skirt and back, releasing feelings she had not come across before. It was exciting and frightening. One arm encircled her, his hand dropping lower, and he pulled her in tightly to his body. That scared her. Father's sermons rolled around her head. She tried to push Mr Cousins off, to speak out, but his tongue was in her mouth. Dropping her head backwards, she said, 'No!' and he laughed as if she was joking. She said it again, and he pulled away long enough to reply, 'Oh yes!' and then she tasted clay as he stuffed a natural sponge in her mouth and pinned her arms. It was the shock more than anything that held her rigid in that moment.

And that was all it took, his trousers dropping to the floor, his hips pinning her against the shelves. The wooden drawing boards digging into her back, her head banging against an upright and then the pain. It shot like a bolt through her but as it subsided, something else happened. She had no choice.

Her hands reached out for him now, her mouth responded to his, she understood his tongue, she pulled at his hips and the colours she saw inside her mind, the waves of nerves that tremored into compulsive response took her away from all the struggles of the world until something came upon her, the like of which she had never felt before and everything—Father, Penny and Becky, and her A levels all juddered into oblivion and she was transported to, to…

The stockroom door opened suddenly.

He was not in her year, but Ellie recognised the boy. His mother arranged the flowers in the church and he stood there, mouth open.

Marcus turned his head.

The boy was gone.

Marcus' trousers were up.

She pulled the sponge from her mouth.

And that was the beginning of the hell.

She is shaking all over in the telling of it. No one has asked her side of the events before. The reality sounds worse than she has led herself to believe.

Loukas says nothing. His silence feels like concern at first and then she wonders if it is disgust. His fingers release hers. Blinking away tears, she looks up at him.

His face does show disgust. She has lost him.

'He was prosecuted? This disgusting paedophile?' he says.

'I was seventeen, nearly eighteen.'

'He was your teacher!' Loukas looks around him, at the people nearby, worried that his words have come out too loudly. His eyes do not rest. Instead, they look from one person to another, losing their focus as he does so until they rest, staring. His fingers clenching into his palm, he cracks his knuckles. Then he calms, looks at her, his hand reaches out, around the back of her neck, and he pulls her head so their foreheads touch.

'Such a thing will never happen to you again. Not as long as I am nearby.' It sounds like a promise as much to himself as to her. The feeling starts like a bubble of wind in her stomach, bouncing, increasing violently before it surges up and fills her chest. Her whole scalp relaxes and there is a sensation of something warm and silky being poured over all her thoughts and worries and memories. The chair she is sitting in is there to support her, the waiter is there to serve her, and she has every right to be in and part of this world.

A small gasp escapes her and tears of gratitude well but do not fall. Could this be love?

'It was terrible afterwards. Accusations, finger pointing, laughing.' It's easy to talk now.

'Shhh.' He puts his fingers to her lips. With no hurry, his lips replace them. She melts into his being and submerges in his love. She knows she has not told him everything but she has told him all the ugly bits, all the parts that disturb her the most, all the bits that would make him run away in revulsion and yet he is still here! She will tell him the aftermath but for now, she basks in acceptance and care.

After what seems like both a second and an eternity, Loukas pays and they wander the streets hand in hand. The shops they look in are of no consequence, the ground under their feet is nowhere near solid. The sky above is vast and blue and they soar with the seagulls.

As the afternoon grows hot, he suggests they go back to the village to sleep, and they take a taxi. But they do not go to the hotel. They are dropped in the square and he leads her up the steep road that she climbed before to sit in the shade of the pines looking over the village.

Leaning back on her hand, her face lifted to the sun, her beauty shines. How strong she is to rise above what has happened to her. Like a phoenix from the fire. A true goddess that the mortals tried to sacrifice. How could she think that what has happened to her would turn him against her?

He moves closer, their arms touching. The village lays sleepy under the blanket of midday heat, and beyond, the land shimmers in the sun but all he can see is Ellie. His arm around her shoulders, his fingers caressing her hair, so warm, so alive.

He is not sure who makes the move first, but her lips are on his again. Her face is in his hands, but her lips are moving fast. Are they eager or are they scared? Pulling away to look in her eyes, he seeks her hands with his own and holds her still. She gets the message. Letting go, she moves slower, as he does. Each moth-like touch is a sharing of tenderness, the delicacy of respect, the gentleness of love. He wants to know her, to give to her but there is no final aim, no conclusive place to which he wants to get. He is fulfilled exactly where he is; it is enough to hold her. That is all the fireworks he desires.

They lay side by side. The heat of the day is making him sleepy and he drifts. With his eyes closed, all he can trust to be real is the sensation of touch, so he explores. His hands, his lips, her hand, her lips, the one becomes the other. His shirt is gone, her shoes kicked off, and he is lost, absorbed into her as she is into him. He offers his care, his strength, his honesty, his truth. In return, she becomes softer, like liquid running warmly through his hands, malleable to his every touch, so precious he feels honoured. Her dress lies amongst the pine needles, his trousers kicked by his shoes, the touch of their skin sending him to fly with the gods, her breath in his ear a thousand secrets of all the past lives they must have lived together. He wants to offer her more, offer all of himself.

With slow movements, they shift and change until, with no expectation or effort, they fuse and at the moment of fusion they freeze, looking into each other's eyes. He holds her gaze to reassure himself that this is what she wants, and the look she returns is asking, no, seeking affirmation that he is playing no game.

'My love, *agapi mou*,' is all he can find to say to express how deep his feelings run and then she moves and he recalls that they are one, the rhythm of life joining them, the mist in his mind swirling. He is on fire. He was born for this moment. The fireworks are there, the lightning, the soaring, the quickening, the anticipation, and then, then he is lost and she is there with him.

A dog barks. Its lonely sound echoes throughout the village. It receives no reply and the cicadas dominate. Seven years cicadas spend in the ground, as grubs, living no life at all, no sun, no warmth, no sight, just existing. That was him. A grub in the ground, just existing. Then the cicada grubs emerge from the ground and they climb, they climb anything they can find, the higher the better, up grass stalks, trees, walls, anything that takes them upwards to the light and there they cast off their old skins, their casings. The eyes uncover, and they can see; their new wings uncurl and they can fly. They are truly alive.

He too can see now; he too has wings now. Like the singing, winged cicada, he is ready to fly.

But unlike the cicada, poor thing, he does not only have a few brief days of summer to find his love and create their children. They, poor ugly bugs, have a few days and then life is snuffed out. That's all the time the cicadas are allotted, then they fall from the trees, they even fall mid-flight. There is no reprieve. But he can fly for decades. They have years to create their children; there is no hurry. There is no need to sing at the top of his voice to find his mate. She is here. But he wants to sing anyway. He wants to shout. To let the world know that he and Ellie have met.

He looks over to her. She is staring at the sky with a smile that reaches her eyes.

'Marry me,' Loukas whispers.

Chapter 16

She laughs, her back arching as she does so. Twisting on her side, she rests her head on her elbow and her merriment fades when she meets his eye.

'You're serious?' she asks.

'I want to spend the rest of my life making you happy. Please give me that chance. I have no ring to offer you, but that is just symbolism. My heart is yours.' Surely she can see his sincerity; surely she must know the depths of his feelings. Otherwise what has just happened wouldn't have happened. She must realise that.

She scrabbles for her dress and wriggles into it without standing up. She seems cross. But why? She feels the same. He knows she does.

'Oh Loukas.' Her voice is gruff with traces of anger. She is on her feet and moving. Scrabbling for his trousers, he stands too, and, jumping to get his feet down the leg holes, he struggles to get them on quickly. He is too slow. Ellie has slipped on her shoes and is running. His shoes are not so easy; the laces will not pull open. He watches her turn into the lane as he gets the first shoe on and, hopping, he tries to get the other one on and run after her at the same time. The pine needles stab at his feet. His toe hits a rock.

'*Agamisou!*' he hisses and falls back, sitting on the springy pine needles, and tears open the shoe, pulling it on. He is up, sees his shirt where he left it, darts back and grabs it and then he is running in earnest to catch up with her.

She is not in the lane. He pulls on his shirt as he is moving. Gravity speeds him to the village centre. She is not in the square. There are voices at Stella's eatery. Maybe she is there. He can ask if they have seen her. If not, he will head to the hotel.

Gasping for breath, hand on knees, he stops in the doorway of the grill.

'Loukas? What happened? Mitsos asks.

'Have you seen Ellie, Mitsos? You know, the foreign girl…'

'Yes, last night she was…'

'No. I mean today. Just now?'

'Calm yourself, my boy. You have lost her?'

'I was just with her and…'

'And how far can someone go? A stranger to the village has not so many choices. Relax, my friend. Have a beer. She will come back or you will find her, but I can guarantee one or the other will happen before nightfall. This is not a big place.' With this, he puts the grill tongs down and opens the fridge door.

'No, no beer. I just need to find her.'

'Why? What's happened? Is she in trouble? She shouldn't be here without her husband. He

187

should be here to take care of her. I told Stella…' He does not finish his sentence.

'What?' Loukas straightens up, getting his breath back, a pain over his eyes. 'I am talking about the English girl. You know, the girl who was here when I delivered the bread yesterday? Ellie.'

'Yes.' Mitsos takes a deep drink of the beer as Loukas tries to make sense of what is being said.

'She is not married,' Loukas states and watches Mitsos, who lowers the beer slowly, making sure he does not meet Loukas' gaze. 'Is she?' Loukas is feeling ever so slightly sick.

'Well, now I am not so sure. It is not for me to say really, but I was not aware that it was a secret. Stella is the one who spoke to her. By email, I mean. But I was given to understand that she was married to a teacher.'

He is going to be sick. His mouth seems to be producing salt; the glands at the back by his tongue pulsate. His stomach is turning. Mitsos puts down the beer and Loukas grabs at it and drinks deeply. The nausea subsides a little.

'Loukas my friend, can I help? What is it?' Mitsos' kindness is ever near the surface, but Loukas runs. Across the square, he sees the old woman, his mother-in-law, coming out of the corner shop. She hails him and waves for him to stop but he has no time now. Pelting past the church, he ducks into the olive grove and heads along the line where olives meet orange trees. There is a smell of goat, but there is no one around. Past old Costas' mud-brick barn, which is being renovated, the outside walls freshly plastered. Even in his manic rush, in some steady and quiet part of his mind, he recalls that once finished, it will be for rent. The trees pass in a blur. The blue of the sea shows between the trunks and then he is out into the forecourt of the hotel.

Now, which room would have the balcony she was sitting on last night? He dashes through reception.

'Loukas?' Sarah stands, puts the phone down, and comes from behind her desk but he is gone, down a dimly lit, air-conditioned, noise-muffled corridor.

All the doors look the same.

The swing doors behind him open. Sarah is following.

'Which one is Ellie's?' Loukas demands.

'What? What's happened?' Sarah is trotting towards him.

'Which one?'

'That one, but she is not there.'

Loukas stops, deflated. He has no idea where to try next.

'Loukas, what is it?' She follows him as he marches back to reception.

'Where's Stella?'

'I think she is in the courtyard with Ellie.'

He knows it is rude to push past Sarah. She has done nothing, but she stands in the direction he needs to go. Three long strides and he swings into the courtyard.

Ellie has a hanky pressed to her eyes. Stella's arm is around her. Sarah comes to a halt behind him.

'You're married!' Loukas barks.

Ellie opens her mouth, takes a breath and wails like a child. Stella rubs her back, making hushing noises.

'And you knew!' he directs at Stella. He has never heard such venom in his voice. He does not recognise himself.

'Loukas, no one tried to deceive you.' Stella begins in Greek. 'I only knew because I asked if she wanted a double room and she said…'

Loukas interrupts her. 'She did.' He points at Ellie. 'She knows how I feel but she did not tell me,' he replies in English. Ellie must hear every word of what he is suffering.

A guest, sitting in a wicker chair in the corner, folds his newspaper as noiselessly as he can and, standing, sidles around the courtyard to make his exit. He mutters 'Sorry' when his arms touches Loukas' as he goes through the arch. Somewhere in a different part of Loukas' brain, a part that has not been scrambled with his life being torn upside down, he makes a mental judgement that the guest must be English. Yes, the English, polite for the insignificant things and silent on the important ones. He slaps his hand on the side of his thigh. One minute his life is complete, his future holds promise, loneliness gone, and the next he is condemned back to making bread for in-laws of a wife he never truly loved, who he

190

was married to for less than sixth months. Life cannot be that unfair. It just cannot.

Ellie does not look up at him. Her face remains in her handkerchief on her knee.

'Loukas.' Stella stands. 'This is not the time and certainly not the place. Come, let us go to my office. We will have coffee. We can discuss.' Again in Greek, as if that is going to help, as if that appeals to the finer side of him.

'I don't want coffee. Coffee is not the answer. She is the answer.' He steadfastly keeps speaking English and points.

'Then let us go and discuss how that is possible.' Stella is calm.

'I would not have unleashed my feelings without good reason to believe they were returned. I would not have even been sure that feelings were there without her direct encouragement.' He cannot stop shouting. Stella has a hand on each of his arms. She is trying to turn him, away from Ellie, out of the courtyard.

He shakes her off.

'Is that what you want, Ellie? For Stella to talk for you?'

Her head remains down.

'Stella, I told you.' Loukas addresses his friend. His rage feels as if it will explode out of him at any moment. 'I told you how I felt and you said nothing.'

That's it! He has had it with them all. All of them are lying and manipulating and secretive and they don't care how much he has been hurt. Natasha may have not been fireworks but at least she was honest. The old woman may be grumpy and mean-spirited, but at least she speaks out and tells nothing but her truth, even if she is wrong.

But maybe she isn't wrong. Maybe her feelings about Stella are justified.

With the hardest look he can manage, he sneers at Ellie and sucks his teeth at Stella. Turning on his heels, he pushes pass Sarah again and strides to the front doors and disappears into the olive grove.

Ellie wails afresh.

'Come, come on.' Stella hooks Ellie under the arm and lifts her to her feet. Ellie complies; there is nothing else she can do. Stella leads her out of the courtyard and into the small conference room that is used for the Greek classes. It is the most soundproofed room Stella can think of, and she must think of her other guests even though her heart bleeds for the young couple. Ellie is leaning on her, sobbing, and Stella guides her to a chair. Sarah has followed them and shuts the door behind her.

'Ellie, my dear,' Sarah begins and finishes by putting her arm around her.

'I told him, I told him what happened. He knows.' Ellie's words come between sobs.

The reception phone rings and Sarah rushes out.

Stella continues to hold Ellie, rock her, stroke her hair. Presently Sarah lets herself back in.

'That was Mitsos,' she whispers 'He said that he thought Loukas was on his way here, that he seemed very upset. Mitsos said he wanted to tell you that he told Loukas that Ellie was married and that he was sorry. He didn't know it was a secret.'

Stella rolls her eyes.

'Ellie, did you actually tell Loukas you were married at any point?' Stella asks as gently as she can.

'Yes, no, not really, but I told him what happened in the store cupboard.'

Sarah looks at Stella, enquiry on her face. Stella shakes her head, lifts her shoulders and lets them drop.

'But did you tell him that you are married?' Stella asks.

'No.' Another wail. The reception bell rings and Sarah leaves them again. 'I told him what was in my heart, Stella. I told him all the truths that felt real. The marriage is like a dream, there is no reality to it. We are in a village I don't really know, with no friends and a man I hardly know who comes home to eat and then he goes back out, comes back, and falls asleep before I have brushed my teeth.'

From her own experience, Stella knows it is best to soothe, agree, and soothe some more. Sarah returns.

'Come,' Stella beckons her in. She would not admit it but she is beginning to struggle with the cultural differences between her and Ellie.

Ellie's distress is bringing back memories of her own. As a married woman, she would never holiday alone, even in her first marriage. She did as was expected, kept up appearances. Even when things got as bad as they did between her and Stavros, she still caused no friction until the point when... She cannot think of that now. Sarah will understand more and her own children must be older than Ellie is now. Suddenly Stella's bottom lip quivers.

'There, there.' Sarah squats by Ellie.

'My marriage was a sham, to stop him getting the sack.' Ellie snivels.

'Oh my,' Sarah says.

'Her teacher,' Stella explains.

'Oh my god.' Sarah's hand goes to her mouth. 'Oh you poor dear.' Her arm is around Ellie. The reception phone rings, and it is Stella who rushes to answer it this time. When she returns, Ellie and Sarah have not moved.

'Mitsos just rang again,' Stella whispers. 'He just saw Loukas go into the bakery, turn out the customers, and close the door on them.'

Ellie wails.

Stella and Sarah look at Ellie, who looks back up with tears running down her cheeks.

'What! What? What does everyone want of me?' She is crying hysterically. 'What am I going to do?'

'So you are back, are you?' the old woman says. 'Kicking customers out and hiding from the world. Kyria Maria from opposite the church saw you in town yesterday with your tramp, as if you were never married. Poor Natasha will turn in her grave.'

'Hush, woman!' the old man says. 'Son, are you alright?'

'The old woman was right: right about Stella, right about the foreign girl, and you were right about women. To hell with them all.' His boots reverberate on the wooden steps as he stomps up to his room. The sound of his door slamming echoes through the building and a picture of Natasha's grandmother shifts to hang at an angle.

Chapter 17

The thought of staying is intolerable. He called her a liar and a slut. Not in so many words, but near enough. She feels like a slut.

Sarah passes her another tissue. She blows her nose loudly and wonders how the body produces so much mucus so quickly. She wipes back and forth and throws the used paper in the bin Stella has provided.

Maybe the people back home were right. Maybe that is just who she is. A tramp! Maybe she should resign herself to it? Hasn't she always felt different; haven't her classmates always treated her as different? Maybe it's true, maybe it is something genetic. If Father knows, that would explain his sermons to her, trying to keep her on the right track.

'Oh God.' She is not sure if she is calling on a deity or blaspheming but really, why should she care? If she is a slut then she might as well be a blasphemer, too. She is already condemned.

'I am a slut,' she mumbles. Stella looks at Sarah for a translation.

'Er, I think... *Poutana,*' Sarah whispers in a low voice.

'Oh no Ellie. No, you must not say this.'

'Ellie, you have met someone who you feel something for. This is not a crime,' Sarah says.

'It is a crime if you are already married,' Ellie mutters. Sarah and Stella do not answer this and fresh tears roll down her face.

'I am thinking that you are who you want to be, at all times,' Stella says. This does nothing to make Ellie feel better, but Stella continues. 'No, you see, we do what is true to our hearts, so if we want to be different, we must change our hearts. I am thinking your heart has changed since you met Loukas, so now you become someone different. This does not make you a *poutana*. Maybe you have just changed.'

'I kind of understand what Stella is saying. It's how you deal with that change that matters now, Ellie.' Sarah rubs Ellie's back, and she lifts her head. She has only been half-listening. If Father gets to know what has happened, part of him will be delighted to be proved right, at the chance for more lectures, pushing her to give in totally to his beliefs, become his puppet. Well, she will not give him the satisfaction. She will not give all those people at school or the press the satisfaction of being proved right. If she goes home now, they need never know about Loukas. There is no one to tell them. It can be as if it never happened and then there will be no ammunition to call her a slut again.

'You make vows when you get married,' Ellie sniffs. 'For better, for worse. That means that no matter what, you stick with your vows, and to do anything else is what makes you a slut.'

'I am not sure that is the whole picture,' Sarah says tentatively after a silence.

'I know it is.' Ellie is emphatic. If she has been born different, if she has been born with this tendency, then she will fight it. This is not about Loukas, it is about deciding who she is willing to be. It is no different than studying to pass exams, giving up smoking, or maybe learning to play an instrument. It will take effort and perseverance and determination, but born that way or not, she will determine who she is.

'I have made up my mind. I need to go home immediately.' Ellie dries her eyes and wipes her nose, sniffs hard and sits up, composed.

'For the record, I am not sure that I think it is a good idea,' Sarah says and Stella nods in agreement. 'If you go without seeing him again, without talking this through, working it out, you may never know if you did the right thing. Do you love your husband?'

Ellie shakes her head. She is quite sure now that she does not, nor ever did she, really, but that is not the point. It is the way she behaves that determines who she is, what she gives into and what she fights. She can see some of Father's sermons now in a different light. She can almost understand them. Not that she wants him to be right; that is not what's important. But whether she loves Marcus or not, she will do the right thing and no one will have the right to call her a tramp.

'You know in your heart when something cannot be saved,' Sarah says. 'It took for my boys to grow and for me to endure years and years of loneliness and an eye-opening holiday here for me to realise. I just wish I had done it earlier.'

'And I will not even "go there", as you British say.' Stella's smile is genuine but sad.

'But I have made a vow. I must stick with my promise.' Ellie's voice is clear and strong.

'Being afraid to break my promise put me in misery for years,' Stella says.

'I just think going back would be the responsible thing to do.' Ellie looks from one woman to the next. They raise their eyebrows and nod slightly but not convincingly.

'Why?' Stella asks.

'Because the way I behave says who I am. Because I am far from home and it is easy to think that this can all be a daily reality, because I don't really know Loukas. Because you just can't up and leave one country and go and live in another.' Ellie starts confidently but her voice wavers as she finishes speaking.

Sarah purses her lips.

'Can and do,' she says.

'Because I am nineteen.'

'That is closer to the truth perhaps,' Stella says.

'What do you mean?' Ellie's eyes widen, alert. Stella and Sarah take a seat around the conference room table. Ellie sits up and faces them.

'How much have you done in your nineteen years?' Stella asks.

Ellie shrugs. She has done nothing. Been to school, taken holidays to Morecambe, but other than that, she has never really left her hometown.

'So how big does this step feel?' Sarah's voice is soft, kind.

'Huge. Too big.' Ellie holds a tissue expectantly to her eyes, but she is not crying now.

'So that is why you feel you must be responsible and grown up. The other way is just too…'

'Scary,' Ellie says, wide-eyed.

Stella wants to hug her, tell her it will all be fine, make everything unpleasant go away, and coo and cluck like a hen, bask in taking care of the girl. The feeling is so strong, she firmly closes her mouth and turns her wedding ring on her finger, thinking of Mitsos and the care he needs. But her urges will not be suppressed so she allows them to manifest by nipping out of the room to get Ellie some water.

Before the door has swung closed, she is back with a bottle of water, wiping the condensation off on her skirt. Ellie takes it gratefully and drinks deeply. Sarah reaches for the air conditioning remote on the table and clicks it on.

'It's just too scary,' Ellie repeats, having drunk half the bottle.

'And the alternative?' Stella asks.

'Go home. Face where I am, see if I can make a go of it, like that friend of yours, Sarah, the old, old woman who had the arranged marriage.'

'Well, I guess you know best,' Sarah replies, convincing no one.

'Only you can decide, Ellie, but if you go, remember that you can always come back,' Stella says.

'Ellie, you are stronger than you think. You will work this out. We have both done it.' Sarah makes eye contact with Stella. 'And we, or at least I, was nowhere near as confident as you are now, nor as smart. You are part of the new generation. You can do homework with your iPod in your ears whilst watching television.' Ellie manages a giggle. 'You have so much clicking in your head that I have no doubt, if you slow down and breathe, you will find your true course.'

'We are all here for you, Ellie,' Stella says, not trusting herself to say any more. There are tears in her eyes.

'I must go, Stella. You have been wonderful, both of you, and I am not ungrateful. It's just that I didn't expect to meet someone like Loukas. I will go, I have to. But I will keep in touch.'

'With me too, please,' Sarah requests.

'Yeah!' Ellie smiles, 'With both of you.' She looks from one to the other.

'So when do you want to go?' Stella asks.

'Today, tomorrow, as soon as I can. It breaks my heart to be here now without him, and I cannot risk seeing him again.'

'Shall I arrange that then, Stella?' Sarah asks and Stella nods.

'But,' Stella says as the door closes after Sarah, 'I insist that you come back in a years' time.'

Ellie agrees. But leaving feels as unreal as staying.

Both of which feel as unreal as returning in a year's time.

Chapter 18

Stella leans back in her chair in her office.

'Why is life never easy?' she asks the chart on the wall. Her heart is with Ellie but her eyes trace the various delivery dates for the things that keep the hotel running smoothly. The people who do the deliveries offer a very comprehensive service. They have a brother who has a laundry so her sheets are in with the deal too, as is the daily bread that comes from a bakery in Saros, run by a distant cousin of Mitsos. It was he who recommended the service in the first place. In truth, Mitsos' cousin's bread is good, but it is not as good as Loukas'. But it was part of the deal, so it is as it is. Anyway, it is a total package and it took away much of the worry in the first tentative weeks of opening the hotel's doors. In the long run, she needs to break that package apart and find cheaper sources for everything.

That's if she can remain open. She and Mitsos had another argument over a troubling letter that came from Saros' planning department. Mitsos immediately started to worry and told her, in unusually harsh terms, that she had taken too big a risk inviting the mayor and his friends to the big opening. She in return made him get his own coffee, which was not kind. She watched him struggle with his one arm and stood by mutely when he knocked over the coffee tin reaching for the matches to light the stove. That was unkind. But the mayor was her hope. That was why she invited him in the first place. She was so sure that he could help with the planning legalisation, oil the way somehow, and on the night of the party, he gave her the impression that he would. But the next day, there was the letter saying that there were irregularities that needed ironing out. It wasn't signed by the mayor, but by some under-secretary. The reality amounted to the same thing.

She felt a bit at a loss for where to turn next. Maybe she should get the local lawyer, Babis, involved, but if she goes down a legal route and it does not go her way, then that is that. It's over. Forever. If she sticks to the personal approach, maybe finds someone else more directly involved in planning, she could smooth the way herself. Didn't Loukas say that his mother-in-law's cousin works in that office? Maybe he could help?

Chapter 19

The rain streams horizontally across the oval window, the thick double layer of glass lending definition to the rivulets. As their speed reduces, the angle of the water steepens until the droplets gather more naturally and run down the glass vertically. Everything beyond the window is grey, the sky a sheet of cloud. The wet tarmac reflects back the runway lights even though it is only mid-afternoon. The tanned passengers, many still in flip-flops and shorts, radiate an air of despondency. The children on board are whining and a baby is crying. Ellie is in the middle seat and the woman in the window seat— two weeks on a beach on Aegina island; the service in the hotel was appalling; there were sea urchins that stopped her going in the water, and every time she ordered a coffee, it was cold—nudges her to start moving, to join the crowd in the aisle, fight to get her bag down from the overhead locker and begin the dash to the bottleneck at passport control.

Ellie would have been even more tired if Mitsos hadn't driven her to the station at Corinth, where the train connects directly to Athens airport. He apologised all the way for letting slip she was married. His English was not very good, so he kept just saying bits in Greek followed by 'sorry'. Ellie tried to reassure him that it was not his fault, that it was never a secret, but she is not sure he understood. Such a sweet, gentle man. Perhaps Loukas will be like him as he gets older. He has the same sort of character.

Mrs Cold-Coffee nudges her a second time just as the seat belt signs are switched off. There is a rush of general movement, so Ellie follows their lead and stands. There is nowhere to go; the aisle is blocked, and now that she is on her feet, there seems little point in standing and she sits again, in the aisle seat.

'It's no good sitting there, dear. It'll be hell at passport control if you don't move yourself. Come on; look lively.' Mrs Cold Coffee's accent is thick, but it is deep, gruff Northern English, not the easy enunciated lilt of Greek. It is a strong accent and familiar to Ellie's ears.

Why do English people that age think they can speak in such an authoritative way to her, to people who look her age? Sarah and Stella didn't. They treated her as an equal, with respect. So did the Greek people she met.

'Lady, where is it you would like me to go? The aisle is blocked.' Ellie decides that she is not going to put up with the condescending way older people speak to her any more.

'Alright, no need to get an attitude,' the woman is quick to retort.

209

'I am not "getting an attitude", I am merely pointing out a fact.' Ellie remains calm.

The woman purses her lips and as Ellie looks back to the aisle, she hears, 'Young people, think they own the world.'

As it is, Ellie's long stride, hurried by the comparative cold, makes her one of the first to passport control, which is absolutely empty but nevertheless corralled so travellers have to zig-zag back and forth across an empty room to make any progress down towards the exit booths. As if to annoy, Mrs Cold-Coffee is one step behind her, almost treading on her heels to push past. Ellie stops, lets her pass, and then ducks the ropes, one after the other to make a direct line to the nearest exit. The passport man checks her ID and waves her through and as she leaves, she can hear Cold-Coffee, who is still zig-zagging down the room, stating as loudly as she dare that the ropes are there for a reason and people shouldn't think themselves so grand as to flaunt the rules. Looking back, she catches a young couple also ducking the ropes as the corral is filling with people behind the complaining woman, whose bag on wheels keeps tipping over to one side and each time, it seems to need more strength than she possesses to right it. It's now her turn to be hassled by the people behind her.

Even this does not make Ellie smile. She may never smile again. She walks straight through baggage reclaim, as she has nothing but her small rucksack containing her t-shirt dresses, her sandals, and her underwear. The decor matches her mood as she passes from one sterile, blank air-conditioned area to another. She follows the signs to the bus station; it will be cheaper than the train. As she steps out of the terminal, the cold, bracing English air hits her. It is still raining. It's always raining.

The bus shelter does little to stop the wind. Hunching in her thin jacket, Ellie reads the timetable. She's just missed the bus, and it will be at least an hour's wait for the next one. She is about to return indoors when a bus pulls up.

'Sorry about the delay. The motorway is at a standstill with this rain.' The driver greets her cheerfully. The inside of the bus is moist with the breath of the other passengers and the steaming of their wet clothes in the warmth. The windows are fogged with condensation and Ellie wipes a hole with the back of her hand to look out at the grey. Grey buildings, grey roads, grey trees, grey people.

The tarmac reflects orange street lights that have come on even though it is nowhere near evening. The sky is one expanse of bruised cloud. The rainwater under the bus wheels hisses and splashes, giving the impression that they are driving up a stream. They build up some speed onto the motorway, where they immediately slow down again. Without the protection of buildings on either side of them, they are even more exposed to the elements. The windscreen wipers thrash back and forth and the water runs incessantly down the glass in a sheet. The driver is hunched forward, peering out into the deluge.

To come back for this! England in the summer! Why? Her heart talks to her but her head is quick to silence it with platitudes about decency, respectability, and responsibility.

The bus continues its crawl through the onslaught. The driver turns up the radio enough for Ellie to hear the travel news. An accident is causing tail backs. There may be a delay of an hour or more, and drivers are advised to use alternative routes. A man at the back of the bus begins to snore loudly. The time passes imperceptibly and the bus slows to walking pace. Ellie almost gives up the will to live.

Hours later, just before they reach the depot where she will have to change to a local bus, the skies slowly clear. Ahead, it is less grim; the blanket above the world softens and lightens but there is still not a touch of blue sky anywhere to be seen.

The local bus is dominated by a party of women returning from a hen night yesterday evening in the city. They are shivering in bunny girl outfits, with orange-peel thighs blue with cold, misshapen acrylic cardigans pulled over their skimpy outfits to cover bosoms squeezing out of sagging cut-away tops and stomachs bulging and rolling as they laugh. There is no longer either will or energy to suck in, no longer a motivation to give the illusion of their bellies being flat. Their voices are loud and coarse. When they alight, the silence brings the focus back to the weather. It has started to rain again.

Ellie is the only person to get off at her stop, which is not surprising.

She passes the patisserie that supplies both the large village and the smaller one. It advertises home-baked bread and cakes, but Ellie suspects the goods in the window are mass produced in Bradford. The crusty bread on display brings a sharp stab of memory of Loukas.

Looking ahead, she purposefully avoids the lane along which Brian lives. Her steps hasten as the road drops into the valley where she crosses the railway line. The slight incline on the other side takes her up to Little Lotherton.

There is a break in the clouds and a patch of blue clears.

Chapter 20

On the corner of the lane she now calls home is an old-fashioned red telephone box. It must be one of a very few left in the country and even more unusual is that it has not been vandalised. Originally, she thought that the majority of the street mustn't have phones, mobile or otherwise, judging by the amount of use it gets, but when she went to use it herself one day, she found that the coin mechanism had been tampered with, meaning that it is possible to make calls from it for free.

Marcus liked that when she told him. He likes all the slightly anarchic aspects of the village. His first real enthusiasm for Lotherton came just after they moved in, when he noticed that the place seemed to attract people who did not want to live in the modern world. Proof of this, he said, was that there were neither satellite dishes nor aerials on any of the roofs, if you didn't count the old couple at the top corner, who have both. A good sign, he insisted, although Ellie had her doubts. She felt that her lack of being part of the world growing up denied her so much useful knowledge. But Marcus was sure it was a positive thing, and so his television remained without an aerial. He did, however, install broadband for his laptop.

Even though the rain has stopped, the cobbles are awash, and the water nearly tops the narrow stone-flagged pavement. There are lights on in almost every house, glowing warm in the bracing wind which now whistles down from the moors, the smoke from each chimney blown flat.

The village seems to have a communal liking for hanging baskets, too. Each door has at least one swinging in the gusts. Those with wooden porches have two, one either side of the door. Window boxes are also a strong feature and in the eerie, white, stormy light, the street is peppered with riots of colour flowers.

The one house that is dark is hers. She pictures the house inside, the warm, earthy colour that they picked for the walls, the plain brick-red throw over the sagging sofa and the piles of cushions on the floor by the open fire. Marcus' abstract art works on the walls, the colours lifting the room, and the rug they found in the attic that covers most of the sitting room floor.

The old metal gate has dropped on its hinges and needs lifting in order to open it. The solid wooden door yields to a kick at the bottom once she has turned the latchkey. It is not that warm inside, which makes Ellie wonder why Marcus has not stoked the Aga. The solid metal wood-burning cooking stove that also heats the water for the central heating is almost cold. Lifting open the stoking door

216

shows that there are only embers in the bottom of the grate. This is unusual. Marcus likes to be warm. Maybe he forgot this morning and has been out all day. Although, judging by the level and the glow of the ashes, it looks as if it wasn't stoked yesterday either.

There is no wood stacked by the stove. Ellie opens the back door, bracing herself for the wind. The small yard at the back opens directly onto the moors. When the wind is really cold in the winter, the sheep press against the house walls, seeking shelter. The gusts take her breath, enter her ears and whip the door out of her hands as she opens it. An armful of wood from under the tarpaulin is enough for now and when she returns inside, the last of the heat has left the one room and she battles, using her whole body, to shut the door. It is not often this windy in the summer, although the rain comes at any time.

The dry wood catches quickly and Ellie opens the vents to give it plenty of air, help it to burn hot. They tend to burn coal on the open fire so once the wood is alight in the Aga, she will use the tongs to take a piece or two over to the fireplace to set some coals smouldering. Once the Aga door is closed, she finally puts down her rucksack, but it is too cold to take off her coat. Instead, she puts the kettle on. She is glad her mother made this contribution to the house. Marcus only wanted to use the wood stove. The water pops and cracks as it heats.

The sink is full of washing up, no surprises there, and the bin is overflowing with beer bottles and pizza boxes. That is not like Marcus. He brews his own beer, is very keen on recycling glass, and very rarely do they have a takeaway pizza. There is wet washing in the washing machine and the drying rack above the Aga is still hung with the clothes she put on to dry before she left. It is odd that she never thought of Marcus as a slob, but maybe she has been too busy trying to be the perfect, newly married wife to find out.

On the wooden kitchen table are flowers she put in one of Marcus' ceramic vases before she left. They have wilted and died and there is a plate with toast crumbs beside them.

The split logs in the Aga are now firmly alight so using the tongs, she takes first one and then a second piece to the fireplace. The chimney draws hard on them and the flames lick up the soot-stained backplate. Careful positioning of the coals ensures they will catch quickly. She also adds more wood to the Aga. It is still not warm enough yet to take her coat off.

When they first moved into the cottage, the whole trip back in time aspect thrilled her. It still does, even though she's cold. But whilst she has been away, it seems something has changed. Something inside her. It is not that she likes Lotherton any the less, rather that she likes the village in Greece more. But no doubt that will fade with time. Already being

218

back in a familiar environment has made the people of the Greek village seem unreal.

The kettle boils, so she makes herself a coffee and wonders what time Marcus will be back. If she is going to make this work, she needs to do it wholeheartedly, forget about Greece. Maybe she should cook. That's a good idea. Wash up, cook, change the linen on their bed. It needed changing before she went away, and it seems unlikely Marcus will have thought about it, if the evidence in the kitchen is anything to go on.

She could also roll the rug back and sweep and wash the flagged floor. Opening the back door always brings bracken and heather dust, bits of bark from the wood pile, and general dirt. If she has time, she will also polish Marcus' mother's brasses that he has lined up on the hearth, which, as usual, is covered in ash. Personally, she hates them but if she keeps them polished, she could use that as a sign that she is on track, thinking straight, making an effort.

'Oh, Loukas.' She stands in the middle of the room and clutches at her chest as if she is having a heart attack. She might as well be, for the pain. She waits for the initial shock of her own outburst to subside and then she rips her coat off and runs upstairs and puts on her warmest jumper, ignoring for the moment the unmade bed. She rolls up her sleeves and heads back downstairs to do the washing up.

Chapter 21

There is a great satisfaction to seeing the house so clean and tidy. The brasses shining, the floor washed. The smell of clean linen drying on the rack above the Aga mingles with the smell of the chicken pieces she took from the freezer and made into a pie that is now in the oven. The house is warming and the bed has been stripped, remade with sweet-smelling sheets, and the washing machine rumbles.

She hung her rucksack on one of the hooks on the back door when she first returned, and there it has remained. She should have put her dresses and underwear in with the sheets, but, like the dirt that collects on the floor and the washing up that grows in the sink, there will always be more laundry.

The sandals come out first along with a trickle of sand that falls to the newly swept floor. It lays golden against the light grey flags. The romance of the sun against the romance of the stark moors. How out of place Loukas would seem here. How inconceivable it is to think of Marcus over there. She puts her sandals alongside the mud-clogged walking boots in the chest by the back door.

Her t-shirt dresses seem unfeasibly thin and flimsy. She wouldn't even wear them to bed in the summer over here. No, that's an exaggeration. She is saying that because of the rain lashing at the windows. In a cloudless moment at the height of summer when the sun has been shining for a day or two and the heather and the peat have soaked up the warmth, there are pockets of sheep-shorn grass between the brackens that trap the heat. She could lay in one of those in these little dresses, smelling the warmth in the undergrowth, listening to the grouse burring and cawing. Invisible from the world. Loukas could lay there too.

Pine needles fall from one of the dresses to join the sand. Burying her face in it, she breathes in its scent, sun cream and pine sap, cotton and Kyria Poppy's shop.

This is not going to make her marriage happen. The underwear in the bottom of the rucksack gets piled into the wicker clothes basket, but the dress she stuffs unwashed into a plastic bag and this, along with the rucksack, is hung on a hook in the cupboard under the stairs in the darkest corner. She needs to forget them, but she cannot wash them, lose the smells, forget the memories. Not yet.

There, she is done. The house is tidy, she is unpacked, the washing is on, the bed has clean sheets and the dinner is in the oven. Now what? What time is it? Surely Marcus should be home by now? The light over the moors, visible through the small

222

window above the deep, chipped butler sink, is fading. The sheep are silhouetted as they come over the rise to the sheltered lee. Maybe Marcus has been staying over at Brian's whilst she was away. But that does not account for the beer bottles and the pizza boxes. He must have been here, and possibly with company.

She could idle her time away on the Internet. His laptop is in its cover down the side of the sofa. It is tempting, but the last time she was on it, she was looking at pictures of Greece and emailing Stella. It will only serve to remind her. She could call Brian, see if Marcus is there, tell him she is home. What is the sensible, responsible thing to do?

Call Brian. Definitely to call Brian and see if Marcus is there.

One glance out of the front window at the water collecting and gushing down the cobbles, the rain pelting against the windows and the wind rattling the gate convinces her she is not going down to the telephone box! She will wait. If he does not come home today, he will come home tomorrow and if he doesn't turn up tomorrow, she will go and call on Brian. He is bound to be there, playing with the trains.

The sofa sinks deeply as she sits. She watches the changing direction of the rain at the window, listens to the wind across the chimney top. The wind chime over the back door is quiet; it must have become tangled.

223

She spots a letter on the mantelpiece, addressed to her, in Mum's writing. Mum has taken to sending her notes since she moved. She says it is because they have no phone. Ellie suspects it is more a result of her being lonely. They never say anything, these letters, they just ramble, cataloguing what Mum bought at the supermarket, things that have happened in the news that need commenting on, the topic of Father's latest sermon. Ellie usually skim-reads them, burns them and, instead of answering them, goes to the phone box and calls. This letter is typical and carries little real news, except Mum mentions that they have taken in a lodger to make use of her old room. This news has an unexpected effect on her. She doesn't mean to, but she starts to cry. It is not so much that she wants to go back there—God knows she doesn't. God knows she never wants to have a Sunday lunch there again as long as she lives, but on the other hand, it would have been nice if Mum had asked if she minded that her old room was to be let out. Not that it is really her room now, but somehow it feels sort of final, as if the choice has been taken away from her, as if she can never go back even if she really needs to. A closed door.

She lets the crying run its course. The initial impact subsides. What has happened fits and feels like a natural continuation of their general disinterest in her. It is probably for the best. Going back would never be a good thing under any circumstances. She flings the letter in the flames and watches it burn.

After a while, she adds coal to the fire, takes the pie from the oven. It is a perfect golden-brown but she is not hungry. The emptiness in her stomach is somehow comforting, friendly, as if Loukas is there with her.

'Stop it, Ellie!' she demands of herself, out loud. Maybe she should clean Marcus' mother's brasses again. Maybe she is just bored. Maybe she should just go to bed.

Next morning, it is as if yesterday's bad weather was just a passing outburst. The sun is out, the clouds are few and fluffy white. The wind has dropped and the world is drying out. The flowers in the window box have lifted their heads and touch the bottom of the window frame with colour. What a difference the sun makes. Opening the back door brings in a smell of warming heath. The tangled wind chime is the only testament to the night before.

She will walk on the moors today. Climb up to the stone circle, past the old reservoir. Or maybe she could sort out the backyard, arrange the wood more carefully, take a load inside and stack it next to the chimney breast. If she sweeps all the bark up, scrubs the winter green off the few flags that nestle by the back door competing with the moors, maybe she could think about putting some sort of seat out there.

No, the moors it will be. She ties the arms of a waterproof jacket around her waist, stuffs a hat in her jeans pocket, wraps a piece of chicken pie in cling film and carefully puts it in the pocket of the jacket and sets out. Maybe she can find a warm spot to read.

These are the sort of days she loves. No thoughts, few clouds, no pressure on her time. She steps lightly over the cushions of heather until she gains a sheep track. She startles one or two of the woolly animals that are chewing noisily nearby, and the way they dart away reminds her of Sarah and her goats.

Ellie consciously tries to concentrate on something else: the bees in the heather, the new shoots amongst the bracken. It works very briefly, but each new focus reminds her of the track on the hillside above the Greek village where she laid, watching beetles scuttle and crickets jump, Loukas by her side.

Her eyes are drawn up to the horizon, but this only serves to bring the old quarry on the edge of the moors into her line of sight. The quarry that is only visible because of the tell-tale line of pine trees around its top edge. She can almost smell them, recall the heat, the touch of Loukas.

'No,' she tells herself and looks back to the path.

Her walk becomes a march and her legs move mechanically and without grace. Her feet stomp and her breathing grows quick. She increases her speed until she stops dead in sight of the stone circle. The ancient rocks stand as tall as a man, some erect, some leaning, only two fallen over. These two lay in the grass, side by side. Like she did with Loukas.

'Oh holy moly, this is not working!' Ellie stops walking and she sits with a thump in the heather, just vaguely aware, but not caring, that she has squashed her chicken pie. What she needs is to stop being in this vacuum. She needs to see Marcus, get back into her old life. As long as she has not seen him, her heart will still be with Loukas. Once she has seen Marcus, it will all be easier. She should find him as soon as he has finished work and suggest that they go to the Shepherd's Arms tonight, even if it isn't Saturday. Maybe at the weekend they can find a ceramics workshop. Perhaps she can broach the idea again about her going to night school to complete her A levels.

The pie has disintegrated into pieces.

'Well, a least the pastry is crumbly.' She forces the optimism and stands to set off back home, scattering the pie pieces for the birds.

Clearing out the backyard keeps her thoughts mostly away from focusing on Loukas for a couple of hours, and when the clock creeps around to the time Marcus usually comes home, she brushes her hair and applies a little makeup. Not much; it is not really her thing. Just enough to give her a glow, a sparkle.

The hands of the clock move so slowly. Marcus does not come. He must be at Brian's.

'Right.' Ellie stands, takes out the remains of the chicken pie that is warming in the oven, and covers it with a towel, pulls on her jacket, bangs the

227

mud off her boots outside the back door and puts them on by the front door, and sets off to Brian's.

Will he be pleased to see her? Or will he be as unruffled as ever? She must think long-term, like the old woman of whom Sarah spoke. If she tries, and keeps trying, love will come. She must picture herself and Marcus as an old married couple with the years behind them, holding hands, loving, close.

Septic Cyril is in the telephone box. He has a bottle of window cleaner and a roll of kitchen paper in there with him and he is cleaning the windows. Ellie is glad the door is shut. Apparently it is not only his house that smells bad. As she passes, Cyril knocks on the glass and grins, peering through his small, round, thick, wire-rimmed glasses. Ellie gives him a little wave and he mists the window he is looking out of with a spray of window cleaner.

She could grow to like the eccentricity of the people here. At least they are not dull.

Halfway down the hill, an old white van coughs and splutters as it begins the climb towards her. In the driver's seat is King Nev, apparently unconcerned by the vehicle's slow progress and worrying noises. By his side is his queen, who waves at Ellie to her surprise, mouthing hello. Queen Helen then speaks to King Nev who smiles broadly at Ellie so she waves at him, too. He waves back.

So after living here for nearly a year, the locals are finally being friendly. About time!

But then, when has she ever been friendly to them? In fact, when has she ever seen them? The first two or three months, she never even went out of her front door, only out the back straight onto the moors. After that, she saw Helen twice, both times in the patisserie, which was the only place she ever went. Both times, Helen quietly said hello, but other than that, when has she even been out to meet any of them? Marcus takes her to do the shopping in his car, and for one hour a week, they sit in a dark corner at the Shepherd's Arms in the next village. Marcus has so impressed on her the need for her to keep a low profile after all that happened that she might have overdone it a bit, perhaps. How different her life would be if she got to know her neighbours, made some friends. Helen and Nev look very nice, smiley, fun. It could be good here.

So, rule one of being back: Go out, use any excuse to go out to places she may bump into people, or they—she and Marcus—could have a party. A housewarming party. Invite the whole street and meet them all. Yes, she will suggest it to him. If he doesn't like the idea, maybe she can do some sort of coffee morning to meet the women like her grandmother used to do in the olden days. She could bake cakes and that sort of thing.

There is a bounce in her step as she heads out of her house, out of her lane and down the hill. The railway line at the bottom marks the official boundary to the next village. Brian's road is the first on the left on the other side of the tracks, defined by a bright yellow front door, on the end of a row mill cottages. There is an alley down the side, which she

229

knows Brian always uses to enter his house by the back door, so she does the same. His handkerchief garden is shaded from wind and weather and faces south. It is a real heat trap and his back door is wide open.

Chapter 22

'Hello, guess who!!' Ellie steps through the back door into the kitchen with a surge of confidence that everything is going to be alright. Even Brian will turn out to not be quite as boring as she remembers him. The sound of the trains whirring reverberates down from the attic.

'Guys?' It is not a house she has spent much time in and she is hesitant, but as Marcus is so friendly with Brian, she supposes she should try to feel more friendly and so, with false bravado, she mounts the stairs, past the bedroom, its door open to a pile of duvet on the unmade bed. The toilet door is also open, and from it comes a strong smell of bleach. The next set of stairs, more vertical this time, go straight up into the attic.

She climbs these stairs slowly and puts her head up through the hole. There is no one there.

The trains are going round and round, but nothing about the track and the model village seems to have changed, which is odd. Marcus said he and Brian were going to rebuild it, and that was why he didn't come home till late every night the week before she went away. Maybe there is a planning stage, maybe they were ordering the stuff they needed. But why would they leave it running, go out and leave the back door open?

Was Brian's car outside? Come to that, was Marcus'? She didn't think to look.

She begins her descent back out of the attic, leaving the trains going. Between the smell of bleach and the bedroom door, there is a muffled sigh from the bedroom. It must be Brian sleeping.

If he wakes up and sees her there, she is going to be mortified. What will she say?

'Oh, so sorry to be passing your bedroom uninvited, Brian, but I have lost my husband.' Or maybe she could play it cool: 'Hi Brian, did you sleep well? Just looking for Marcus, creeping about your house, uninvited.' No, that would be too weird to contemplate! Maybe the bathroom has a window, maybe she could... No, she is being ridiculous. What is the responsible and adult thing to do? Knock. Yes, why not? Knock on his bedroom door, explain the back door was open, and ask if he has seen Marcus.

That's what she will do. That, or she will crouch down as she passes the door so he will not see her beyond the end of the bed and she can sneak back down the stairs and out the back door.

The floorboard she steps on creaks. She freezes and closes her eyes, stops breathing. There is another sigh and then a half snore. She takes another step, another creaky board. As she nears the bedroom door, she flattens herself against the wall. She will peek through the crack between the hinges of the

233

door, and if he looks safely asleep, she will tiptoe out. If he is awake, she will knock with aplomb and brave it out.

The crack of the door is wide enough and in amongst the mess of duvet, she can see Brian's blond hair. He is lying face down, both arms stretched out above his head. He looks quiet sweet when he is asleep, nice looking even. Younger than Marcus.

She watches him for a moment, encouraging positive feelings towards him, telling herself that he is not boring. He is a good friend to Marcus. There's a grunt and the bedclothes move.

It happens so fast, it is not real. For a moment, she does not respond. Her limbs do not react. Then she moves quickly.

'What the…' The words come out like one of the screeching grannies in Greece, so high-pitched and Brian pushes the side of his face into the pillow, but his hands remain above his head. She stands squarely in the doorframe. Brian's eyes swivel toward her, open and wide, but he makes no attempt to turn onto his back and face her. But it is not Brian she is looking at.

Marcus lifts his head and turns to face her, wipes off the spittle on his lips with the back of his hand. 'Ellie?' He almost giggles the words. No shock, no remorse, nothing, just as if her being there is a bit of a funny joke.

'What…' Ellie tries again. Marcus sits up, leans back against the headboard, his chest hairs glistening with sweat. Brian cowers lower into the pillow as if he is wishing it would absorb him.

'Did you find yourself, Ellie? Did you grow, experience, experiment?' Marcus takes the remains of a hand-rolled cigarette from the ashtray by the bed and lights up. He takes a long drag while Ellie stands there with no idea what to say or do. It feels impossible to move. All she can do is watch. With one hand, Marcus leans over Brian and undoes a loose black band that until that moment, Ellie has not noticed.

Brian pulls his hands down from above his head quickly as they are released, casting off the bonds, and reaches for the cigarette that Marcus is drawing deeply on, sucking air in with the smoke and holding it before exhaling at length. He gives the remains to Brian, who has hidden as much of himself as he can under the duvet. Just the two fingers holding the cigarette and his face are visible. Ellie continues to stare. One drag from Brian and the cigarette is down to the butt. His mouth dips under the duvet; leaving just the fingers waiting for Marcus to take the glowing end, and a pair of wide scared eyes.

There is nothing she can do but stand there. She seems to have lost her senses. A ringing in her ears is matched by specks of light that spin before her eyes. Her mouth is hanging loosely open and there is a vague feeling that she might be dribbling. Her legs have locked and will not respond and her hands have gone numb. If she could be granted one wish, it

235

would be to be able to move, to run, to take this sight away from her, to be somewhere, anywhere else. On top of the moors, fighting the rain, throwing stones at a goat, anywhere but here.

Marcus takes the cigarette end, drops it in the ashtray, and folds his arms across his naked chest, relaxed, unruffled as always.

'Well?' he asks her with the air of a teacher waiting for an answer. Then she is released and everything moves at once. She trips over her own feet in her rush for the stairs, bangs her head against the top newel and sinks to the floor.

'Ellie, you alright?' Marcus calls after her and she can hear the rustle of bedclothes. On her feet again, she takes the steps as many as she can at a time. Holding tightly to the banister, she leaps the last four, sprawls on the floor but grovels on her hands and knees to stand and continues to run.

'Ellie, El, hey. Isn't this what life is about? Exploring, learning…' She can hear Marcus' tread on the stairs.

Flinging the back door shut behind her, it slams—but not loudly enough, and the shattering of the glass in its window is not nearly enough damage.

Now her legs won't stop, her feet pounding the pavement, past the patisserie. Past the travel agents, they don't stop until she is back at the main road, and it starts to rain. As she speeds past shops and houses one hand scrabbles in her back pocket, for reassurance that the thin booklet that gives her some security, that gives her hope is there nestled next to her credit card. If she was not out of breath she would sigh with relief.

Then, of course, it starts to rain! What else would it do? What else can she expect? Becky and Penny are no doubt off to university, her parents have a lodger for her old room, she has blown it with the guy of her dreams, her husband is shagging Brian the boring history teacher, and she is standing in a busy road in the rain! Of course!

With hair plastered to her head, she looks up to the skies, lifting away strands that cling to her cheeks. The rain hurtles at her like stair rods now, an infinite number of spears, as if nature herself wants to impale her. Leaning against the sharp edges of the dry stone wall that borders the pavement by the road, it seems hardly worth taking another breath. The jagged edges of the granite dig into her back. There is her and there is the rest of the world, and the rest of the world looks intent on squeezing her into the outer darkness, denying her a place, robbing her of any comfort.

The cars that speed by throw up spray, the drivers seeing her too late to slow down and reduce the arcs of water that reach the pavement. The first drenching is a shock, the cold biting her skin but then that too fits with her life. What has she left? She may not technically be homeless but she has no home to go to. Her existence is loveless. If she disappeared from this spot, it would alter no one's life. She could just climb over the dry stone wall, crouch down in

the shadow it casts, out of sight of the cars, and wait
for hypothermia to end her miserable little life.

Chapter 23

'So you ask no one if you can take the bar job but you storm back in here, throwing customers out, and expect your place to be waiting for you as if you were never gone?' The old woman flings these words at Loukas as he slams the bolt home on the inside of the shop doors.

'Don't start, old woman. I am in no mood for your tongue.' Loukas faces her, meeting her gaze, staring back, letting the anger in his eyes show until she has the sense to back down.

'Steady...' the old man mutters.

Loukas turns his steady look on him. 'Or what, old man?' The title Loukas uses to address his father-in-law is laden with sarcasm. 'Will your old body straighten and life come to your limbs so you can whip me like I am a child?' Loukas pushes past them both. In the kitchen, he yanks open the oven to find it is bare. There is a loaf of *tsoureki* on the table. The old woman hurries in at the sound of the oven door.

'The *tsoureki* is for...' she begins, her hands reaching towards it, but Loukas is there first.

He says nothing, ripping off a big piece and stuffing it in his mouth to make his point that anything they have to say has no meaning for him. He takes the old man's bottle of ouzo from the shelf above the sink. The old man is also in the kitchen now and he hurries to open the cupboard where the glasses are kept, but Loukas leaves the room, bottle and sweet bread in hand. The house resonates with his boots on the wooden stairs, and the bare bulb hanging from the kitchen ceiling swings in response to the slam of his bedroom door.

Stella arrives back at the eatery in the village to hear a door slam somewhere in the closed depths of the bakery. The raised voices of the old man and old woman sound through the muffle of the walls. They are arguing. Having left Ellie to sleep with Sarah looking in on her, she wonders if there is anything she can do right now. The eatery, in comparison to the rest of her life and the turmoil in her head, is pleasantly calm. The farmers are talking in a hushed, lazy tone that suggests they have already eaten. Mitsos is scraping the black burnt bits from the grill.

'Here comes trouble,' Iason calls through to them, looking out of the eatery's open door. Stella follows his gaze but she is at the wrong angle to see anything. She steps back from the fridge that she is restocking to look out of the double door in the grill room.

The old woman trundles with purpose across the road towards her.

'Stella!' The old woman stands, hand on thin hips, her cheeks sucked in, lower jaw pushed out, brows lowered. 'Come here, we speak!'

Stella wipes the condensation off her hands with a tea towel.

'Easy, Stella. Don't let her get to you,' Mitsos says.

But she feels no unease. She was taunted and bullied all her childhood, and this old woman holds no fear for her.

'What do you want, Stheno?' Stella faces her, still wiping her hands in the sunshine.

'You did this. You and your swanky hotel.'

Stella does not feel the need to reply.

'Well, are you happy now?' The old woman waits for a response. Stella's instinct is to turn on her heel and continue restocking the fridge, but this will only inflame the situation.

'What do you want from me?' She speaks quietly.

'What do I want from you? Ha! I want nothing from you. Nothing, not even if you beg! You are not content with bullying the people of the village to run around for the crumbs thrown to them from your business, your hotel, what with hinting you will take rental cars from the garage and selling olive wood bowls to the tourists, you make yourself even more grand by upsetting and snubbing people that you have no use for. What right do you have to

242

interfere into peoples' lives as you do? Well, you may find your life is not so easy.'

Stella sighs and her shoulders slump. She has heard this all before, but she really thought the last of the villagers would have got past all this by now.

Her poor Greek baba would turn in his grave. How he had tried to protect her all his life, even on her first day at school! But children can be cruel and it seems some never grow up.

Stella recognises now that the village eatery was her first attempt at trying to contribute to the village, in part an offering to buy her redemption for having a gypsy mama. It altered a good many people's minds, mostly those of the hungry farmers, but it has not been enough. Still there are those with these streaks of bitterness which they occasionally throw at her.

The hotel, which Stella considers as her biggest offering to this community, is likely to be her last. She has no energy for any more. From now on, they must take her as they find her. The hotel offers work to a number of local businesses. The garage, the wood carver, the beautician, the hairdresser. It will bring more tourists into the village, so the corner shop and the kiosk will benefit. If the stubborn villagers cannot see who she is and how her heart beats by now, they never will. They are remaining stubborn out of pride. She cannot alter that and would be a fool to try.

Nevertheless, Stheno's words sadden her. But other than that, they have little effect. She has heard

243

it all before and the threats the baker's wife is making are hollow, hot air. She has no real ammunition. But it is utterly demoralising to hear Stheno use the hotel, the very things she is offering to the village, against her.

She waits till the old woman subsides and then looks her in the eye.

'Life has never been easy, so what threat is this?' Stella's words are calm.

Stheno's puckered mouth opens and then closes and Stella turns away and continues to refill the fridge. It is only by the flapping of the old woman's slippers across the road that she knows Stheno has left.

Chapter 24

'How are you doing here?' Stella addresses Mitsos as she enters the eatery again. She stuffs a bunch of papers detailing the illegalities of the hotel, which she was studying on the way over, back in her pocket. The less Mitsos knows about it, the better. He has a tendency to become anxious.

'I forgot to order that charcoal the other day. Do you think that we will be alright if we get some brought over tomorrow?' Mitsos' eyebrows are raised and worried lines wrinkle his forehead. Stella looks in the bag by the grill and nods. There is enough for today. Whilst she is standing close to him, he says quietly, 'I really messed things up, didn't I?'

With the hotel foremost in her thoughts, Stella hesitates before realising to what he is referring.

'No, Mitsos. It wasn't you. I should have told Loukas, I even tried to, in an indirect way, but it was Ellie's place to make her position clear.' Stella looks over to the closed bakery. 'Anyway, he is blaming me now, not you.'

'That's not good.' Mitsos puts two sausages onto a plate which looks bare without the usual hunk of bread. 'Lemon sauce?' He shouts through to the customer in the adjoining room. Interpreting the grunt of a reply, Mitsos liberally pours on Stella's homemade sauce before wiping his hand on his apron so as to take a firm grip on the plate to take it through. On his return, he adds more sausages to the grill.

'Anyway, Sarah says she can come back, after taking the goats out, for an extra two hours to serve on the beach bar tonight, but she doesn't know how to mix a cocktail,' Stella says. 'I have someone else who will come in to do a couple of hours before that but later on, I'll go back and do it myself.' She leans her elbows on the counter, her head in her hands. It is just possible that the hotel is more than she can handle. If she cannot get the staff and the papers, then what? The place will have to close. It will be worthless and their savings will be gone.

'You cannot do everything yourself,' Mitsos says kindly, as if hearing her thoughts as he steps from behind the grill to embrace her in a one-armed hug.

'Right now there is no choice, and besides, it is not as if the bar is a real problem. Another barman is not so hard to find.' She rests comfortably in his embrace, soaking up Mitsos' love, offering hers in return. He is the most important thing. Forget the hotel, forget the money. A twinge of sadness shadows her thoughts as Ellie comes to mind. 'It will be harder for Loukas to find another Ellie, and Ellie her Loukas,' she says reflectively.

247

'Have a little faith in life, Stella. Look at our paths. They were harder but we still found each other.' Mitsos' chin rests on the top of her head.

'Yes, but how old were you?' Stella laughs quietly, intimately, as Mitsos bends his head to lean his forehead against hers.

'Well, I had to find some wisdom and courage first. Without those, I would never have found you,' Mitsos declares and kisses the end of her nose.

'Is this a dating agency or can a man get a meal here?' Iason wipes his bald head with a handkerchief as he enters.

'From what I hear, you don't come here to eat these days, Iason my friend.' Mitsos pulls away from Stella and goes back around the counter, colour flushing to his cheeks.

'Is that right, and why else would I be coming here?' Iason takes a beer from the fridge.

'To save your voice.' A farmer from the next room shouts into them. Iason leans through the adjoining door to see who is speaking.

'Ah it's you, neighbour!' There is laughter in Iason's voice.

'Who else would know your business?' comes the reply.

'Anyone with ears,' a new voice joins in. 'Morning and night, you shout at that poor boy.' Both sympathy and teasing are mixed, in equal measure, into the way this is said.

'Is he actually looking for a job?' Stella asks.

248

'The boy's fussy. I tell him he cannot afford to be fussy. I told him to take your bar job but he refuses.' Iason takes a napkin from the counter, this time to wipe the back of his neck, and then he ducks through the doorway to be greeted by some well-meaning banter.

'It's harder for the young these days,' Stella observes to Mitsos.

'It never occurred to me that I would do anything different from my baba,' Mitsos agrees. 'Choice can be very distracting and stop you from getting on with life.'

'I think life happens when you are distracted by making choices,' Stella says.

'Well, one thing's for sure, none of us end up where we expect to be.' Mitsos lifts the chips from the fat, gives them a shake and pours them into a dish. 'Can you take those through?' When Stella comes back in, Mitsos asks, 'So will you be very late?'

'Probably.'

'It was my dream at one point, you know, when I was about Loukas' age, to run a beach bar.' Mitsos sighs and nods as he looks at his arm that is not there.

'Everything alright?' Stella greets Sarah, who is busy drying up glasses.

'Yes, fine.'

'Did you have to mix many cocktails?' Stella asks with a smile. She had printed off some basic cocktail recipes, stapled them together, and put them behind the bar for Sarah just in case. In the sand around the bar, there are many cigarette ends. That's another job for which she must find a solution. The beach must be clean.

'Oh no. Everyone's been drinking beer or fresh orange juice.' Sarah seems buoyant but looks tired. Stella knows she will also have to find another receptionist to job share with Sarah if she wants things to run smoothly. There is so much to think about suddenly.

'An easy shift then,' she replies lightly, keeping her worries to herself as usual. It would be nice to share but then, her problems are her own, so what's the point?

'Yes. Oh, and a man I didn't recognise who said he was from planning was down here looking around.'

'Oh, did he leave a name, say what he wanted?' She doesn't manage to keep her voice calm now.

'No.' Sarah stops what she is doing to look up. 'Stella, what is it? Is there a problem?'

'There is a slight hiccup, shall we say, with planning.' How much should she share?

'Oh, but everything is illegal here. I thought you Greeks were used to that!' Sarah chuckles.

'It's difficult to be legal, that's true. Too many laws cross over each other. You stick with one and you break another.' Stella tries to make light of the conversation but the tension in her voice cannot be hidden. 'But this one with the planning could be a big problem. I will go into Saros tomorrow find out who it was and who really has the power there.'

'It'll be the mayor surely,' Sarah says, laying her tea-towel flat on the bar. Even in the relative cool of the evening, it will dry quickly.

'Yes, but the mayor said he was all for the hotel on the opening night and, with these local issues, everything can be overcome if everybody is willing. So that means someone somewhere is not willing. If I can find out who, find out why, then I can resolve it.' She smooths out the tea towel Sarah put down.

'I wish everything was fixable.' Sarah takes her bag from under the counter and joins Stella in front of the bar. 'I suppose it's too soon for you to have heard anything from Ellie yet?'

Stella nods and looks out to sea as far as she can. Somewhere out there across the waters, poor Ellie is trying to make a bad marriage work. She feels for her. Maybe she will email her. She won't have time today, but tomorrow, after Ellie has settled back into her life a little.

'There was a couple down here earlier. I don't know them, but you will. A tall man with a blond woman with hair extensions, long nails. The one who looks a bit out of place for the village,' Sarah says.

'Ah, probably Magdalene, the girl who worked on the television for a while.'

'Oh did she? I didn't know that. Anyway, I think they thought I was Bulgarian or Polish or something and couldn't understand because they chatted away in English, here at the bar, as if I didn't exist.'

'He is half-Canadian.'

'Oh, I did wonder why they weren't speaking Greek. Anyway, it seems, their house backs onto the bakery.'

'Yes I know,' Stella says absently, still distracted by the thought of someone from planning nosing about whilst she was not there.

'Right. Well, apparently Loukas, presumably straight after he left us here, went back to the bakery and was screaming at his in-laws. Then he stole a *tsoureki* that was on order for her, this Magdalene, and he also took the father-in-law's ouzo bottle up to his room and about ten minutes later, he brought it back down empty, only to take a full bottle up. They were talking about him, saying he was banging and crashing about until the early hours. Apparently, he didn't get up to make the bread…'

'I know. We've had none in the eatery today,' Stella says.

'And this morning, they found the second bottle, empty, in their flower bed beneath his window. So I guess he is taking it hard.'

'I imagine it is just as hard for Ellie.' She looks at her watch. Maybe she could stop and email her right now.

'Anyway, that's the news, but I really need to get going if I am on reception tomorrow morning, so are you alright to take over now?'

'Yes sure,' Stella says, but now she is worrying about Ellie and Loukas too. Maybe she should not have let Ellie go. She could have stayed and worked out whatever she and Loukas had together. Maybe letting her go was the worst thing to do.

'...and tonic water,' Sarah finishes, but Stella was thinking about Loukas drowning his troubles in an ouzo bottle. That is not a good thing. Not good at all.

Loukas lifts his head from his pillow. The evening is still too bright. When it grows really dark, he will go into Saros, find a bar, maybe find some girl, any girl, and together they will drink the night away. He reaches for the ouzo bottle and then vaguely recalls he threw it out the window. The picture of Natasha smiles angelically from her photo frame by his bed. It is the last face he wants to see. He purposefully knocks it over, so it falls face down, but the table is too small, the weight unbalanced, and it falls to the floor. The sound of cracking glass does nothing to lift his mood. His sister continues to stare from her frame, unmoved.

At first he was angry with Ellie. She played with him, tortured him, teased him. A rich English tourist coming to his country for a bit of fun, to take her mind off her own troubles. She used him. Strutting around in that little t-shirt dress, showing her legs, leaving little to the imagination. How was a good Orthodox boy meant to deal with that?

The anger was fuelled by the ouzo. It grew into hatred; for her, for his mother-in-law, for Stella, for Natasha. If Natasha had been more like Ellie, none of this would have happened. Then the hatred turned inward, for his naïvety, his stupidity, his vulnerability, for Stella's not taking care of him, for her introduction in the first place.

Now, with the ouzo all gone, the bread unmade, and the hours passing, his mood has become heavy, draining sadness. He has no future in the village making bread; any fool could see that. But neither has he a future in Athens, with his baba's business gone. His mama holds everything together with a couple of hours a day making the beds in a fancy hotel that has recently open near the house in Gazi. A job in a beach bar in a hotel can only be seasonal and he will be forever surrounded by Ellie types. English girls looking for fun.

He could play that game. Hit on the older ones maybe, accept presents. Why not; he is no more important to them than a new purse or ring or something. Just a thrill for the moment, quickly losing its attraction.

He turns onto his back. The cracks in the ceiling are too familiar. How many hours over the last year has he stared at them, wondering about his future, only to fall asleep and wake with his mother-in-law's rapping on the wall? At least the bakery is safe. If he was satisfied with that, he would never have noticed Ellie. But now that he has, the bakery is not enough. The circle of thoughts is driving him mad. Getting up, he pulls on his trousers, puts back on the same shirt he wore yesterday, and experiments with standing vertically. His head swims.

Chapter 25

Having started in the bars in the main square of Saros town, Loukas now slinks his way towards the backstreet bars. His shirt is hanging out of his jeans on one side and there is a wobble to his walk. The moon is bright but the occasional streetlight helps. The jasmine is releasing its fragrance and the day's heat is absorbed in the walls and the pavements cocooning those who are out, slowing their pace. As it is a weeknight, the Athenians are not filling the bars. Occasional tourists brighten the pavements in acid-coloured summer wear, but mostly it is quiet.

The next bar is small. A converted narrow, downstairs room in one of the old houses, the plaster on the walls uneven, the wooden beams exposed and darkened with age. The counter is at the far end, modernised with a blue neon light under the drinks shelf behind. Four cheap wooden stools are lined up in front of a shelf that serves as a place to put glasses, ashtrays, and bowls of peanuts down one side. There is no more room for seating or tables than this. Above the shelf hangs a framed poster of a Greek man in a sharp suit, bow tie dangling and a bottle of Metaxa brandy in one hand. He strolls down his black and white street in nineteen-fifty-something, happy with just the bottle as his companion. Loukas understands how he feels. He slithers onto a stool, ignoring the only other customer who has chosen to sit next to the bar.

The bartender, unshaven, slightly pudgy, puts a fresh bowl of peanuts down in front of Loukas and waits for his order.

'Ouzo,' Loukas snarls.

The man on the stool by the bar looks over to him. When the ouzo is served, it is placed on a mat on the shelf with a small bowl of ice and a spoon, sunk into the melting cold.

'Put that on my tab,' the man on the next stool says loudly. 'How are you doing, Loukas?'

In the village, he expects it. Everyone knows everyone; the *kafeneio* there is an extension of home, the streets an extension of the yards, families intermingled for years. There is no privacy. But here in Saros, he was hoping, nurturing the slightest possibility that he could, for a few hours, be invisible. Why can it not be like the anonymity of Athens, so he is lost in the sea of faces, left alone? With lazy effort, Loukas takes the time to look up at the man.

He has no idea who he is and searches the face to try to recognise some aspect but draws a blank and raises his eyebrows to say so. Whoever it is, he is not much older than Loukas, with thin, lank hair that needs attention. He's obviously spent time waxing it rigid, but it does not look good. The man's suit is cheap and too big at the shoulders but his white shirt is ironed, so someone is taking care of him. A mother, an aunt? He doesn't look the married type.

'Vlassis!' The man introduces himself, patting his chest with a flat palm, bitten fingernails on display. He raises his glass with his other hand to salute Loukas.

Loukas still cannot place him, lifts his glass in return, but says nothing.

'Vlassis!' He says again. The barman watches the exchange from behind his counter, wiping out the inside of glasses with a crisply laundered tea towel.

'Vlassis Tavoularis,' he expands, but Loukas shakes his head. He neither knows him nor cares.

Usually he doesn't take ice in his ouzo, preferring the drink's warmth undiluted. The name Tavoularis sounds familiar. He plops a second ice cube into his glass.

'Tavoularis?' he asks slowly, a dull recognition fighting to the front of his messy thoughts.

'Yes.' The man grins at him with relief at being identified.

'It took me a moment,' Loukas says, but he cannot rouse much enthusiasm.

'How are they?' Vlassis tone becomes sober. 'Such a shock to you all, my sympathies to you. I have not seen you since the funeral.'

Loukas does not want to talk about Natasha, her death, or her funeral. But the man continues, intent of conversation.

259

'Aunt Stheno has got in touch with me since you know, a few months ago, but I have not seen her recently. Is she alright?'

'She's fine.' Perhaps it is time to go to another bar, drain this ouzo and walk out. The last thing he wants to talk about is the old man and old woman, but what else has he in common with this man, whom he recognizes now as the old woman's nephew.

'Yes, I was surprised when she got in touch after the funeral. I think you know she has not been close to my mama for some years?'

Loukas nods numbly.

Vlassis raises a finger at the barman, who comes from behind his counter to pour two more ouzos. Loukas almost puts his hand over the top of his glass to refuse, so he can leave. But then, a free drink is a free drink.

'My mama was pleased, as well you can imagine. But it was me that the old woman got in touch with.' There seems to be some pride in this statement and Loukas turns his head to take a lazy look at Vlassis' face to see if the egotism shows there too. It does.

'I don't know if you have heard or not…' Vlassis sits up on his stool, smooths the front of his shirt, and adjusts his jacket to sit better. 'I am doing well in the mayor's office, Assistant Deputy Planning Officer.' Loukas catches Vlassis looking at his own reflection in the glass of the framed print on the wall.

His chin lifts a little higher as he runs a hand over his anointed quiff.

'My congratulations,' Loukas replies automatically.

'Yes. Mind you, it is a lot of work. Many late hours.'

'I bet you have to do the work of every one of those lazy fat cats above you,' the bartender chips in. 'Two years it took for the planning to come through to change use of this place. To open it as a bar.'

Vlassis colours in a second. A piece of his slicked-back hair falls over his eyes in an unbecoming curl as he turns his head sharply to face his accuser. 'It is a very busy department,' he defends. 'And yes, I carry a lot of the workload.'

'I know. I see the Deputy Planning Officer and the Planning Officer sitting in the *kafeneio* opposite most of the day.'

'I think they hold their business meetings there…' Vlassis stutters slightly.

The barman chuckles and Loukas snorts into his glass.

'Well, your mother-in-law knows the extent and power of my position,' Vlassis says sharply to Loukas.

The barman disappears behind a curtain to one side of the shelves behind his counter, leaving his customers alone. Loukas drops in an ice cube and watches the clear liquid turn opaque. He swirls the cube round with his finger that he then sucks. He will drink this and go, but something about what

261

Vlassis is saying niggles him. It has been an hour or two since he could think clearly but somehow, this one-sided conversation feels like a dangling key to his future. He can feel the connection but he cannot see it. Metaxa and Ouzo have never mixed well. He should know that by now and have stuck to ouzo.

'Power?' Loukas summarises Vlassis' sentence into one word so he can absorb it.

'Yes, power.' Vlassis has not recovered from the barman's slight. His voice still bristles.

'Power,' Loukas repeats. It is all he is capable of now.

'Yes, some people think they have the power, but they don't. They flash their money about, trying to be better than everyone else, showing off and becoming like queens and walking all over good, honest, hard-working people. Honest people like your in-laws.'

Loukas opens his mouth to protest how little work his in-laws have actually done over the last year but then the Metaxa in his bloodstream convinces him that silence would be the easier option, so he shuts it again.

'Queens,' he murmurs instead, and an image of Ellie comes to mind.

'Yes, queens. The old woman says she struts about like a queen.'

Loukas blinks hard and turns to face Vlassis. Why would he say Ellie struts like a queen, how would he even know her?

'She's not even Greek, you know.' Vlassis leans towards him and speaks in hushed tone. 'She is gypsy stock.' He takes a handful of peanuts and throws one in the air and catches it in his mouth.

'Who are you talking about?' Loukas asks, his words slurring one into another.

'That woman who did not give you the bread order for her flashy hotel. Why, who did you think I was talking about?' Vlassis throws another peanut. It misses his mouth and lands in his ouzo. 'She thinks she has it all, but she is not the one with the power. I am.' And he downs the last of his ouzo, slaps Loukas on his back as he stands.

'I'll make sure you and the old woman are alright, Loukas. Trust me.' As the barman returns, Vlassis leaves, and it takes a moment for Loukas to realise he has not paid. But the barman does not charge Loukas. Instead, he writes down the amount Vlassis owes in a big book that he draws from under the bar and when he has finished scribing, he shuts it with a thud.

'He will be back tomorrow. Same time every night. Always alone,' the barman confides. 'His bar tab keeps me going during the week. But don't get me wrong, I am pretty sure it is not his need for alcohol that keeps him coming back. He is just lonely. He stays longer and drinks less the more people are here.' His laugh is short but uneasy.

It is night now and the sky is a deep inky blue. Loukas walks with his head back, hands in pockets. Somewhere, far away, if Ellie is looking up, she will be seeing the same stars.

'Damn you, Ellie,' he mutters as he staggers to the next bar. His conversation with Vlassis lingers.

Ellie hunches on the other side of the dry stone wall along the main road in an out-of-the-way part of Yorkshire. It is hard to believe that yesterday, she was too warm even in the lightest of clothing. The rain is coming down at such an angle that it is dry where she sits, but this is little consolation, as she is already soaked through. She feels as miserable on the outside as she does on the inside. It shouldn't take much over an hour or two with the cold wind for the onset of severe hypothermia. First, she will continue to shiver as her body fights to keep her internal organs warm, then she will become confused, and finally, a warmth will seep over her. She will feel cosy as she falls into unconsciousness and her pulse will weaken until it stops. Not such a bad way to go. Her tears mix with the rain.

What on earth has she really just witnessed at Brian's house? Was that a relationship, a fling, a moment of drunkenness in the middle of the day? The way they were with each other, so familiar, like they knew what each other would do next, Brian waiting for Marcus to take the cigarette end. Was it even a cigarette? It smelt odd.

How long has it been going on? The whole time they have lived there? And who knows? Maybe the whole of Lotherton knows and maybe that's why

Helen and Nev smiled. Maybe they are laughing, maybe the whole finger pointing is about to start again.

There is no reason not to, so Ellie opens her mouth and wails with the wind and the rain. She could not bear to go through that again.

Or is she being childish? Maybe experimenting, exploring is what life is all about. Maybe Marcus is right: maybe all adults do this sort of thing and they just keep it quiet from the children.

But that's ridiculous. Mitsos would never explore away from Stella, not with anyone. It just isn't in his nature. Nor would Sarah. She only had one man in her heart and she was even waiting for him.

It seems everyone has someone, but who can she turn to? Sarah and Stella said she always has them but they are over the other side of the world. Then again, so what, why should she not go back to where someone seemed to actually care about her?

Loukas, that's why.

At the base of the wall is a small fine pile of soil next to a hole thin enough to poke a blade of grass in. At the moment, it is filled with rain water. In a sheltered, bracken-free spot that she found last summer up on the moors was a similar hole and she spent a couple of hours watching the industrious ants come and go. Some just marched; others hauled seeds and bits of dead insects four and five times as big as their own segmented bodies. There are no ants today, it's too cold and wet. The ants in Greece were so much bigger and warmer!

'Loukas.' Ellie whispers his name out loud through chattering teeth. She lifts her head and looks up at the horizontal javelins of rain. He showed such care about what had happened to her in the stockroom. He uttered such supportive words. Her family, her peers, and the papers did nothing but throw their own javelins, spears of snide remarks, unthinking humour and downright nastiness. The only thing that stood in her way was her marriage to Marcus.

'What marriage?' Ellie spits and wipes the rain from her face. Marcus has broken all his vows. He has broken the promises he made and reduced their marriage to a falsehood.

'There is no marriage!' Ellie says bitterly. She repeats the phrase in her head, again and again to take it in, and with it comes a slow realisation.

'There is no marriage!' This time, the words hold joy. She stands shivering, face to the rain, shouting to the heavens.

'There is no marriage.' A sense of freedom surges through her. She climbs the wall and jumps down to the pavement on the other side.

Why on earth has she been sitting here waiting to die when, with an explanation, she could be in Loukas' arms?

Her knee-jerk reaction to Brian and Marcus was to run, hide, wishing for her world to stop as if she is without power—as usual, just as she has been taught. But that is not who she wants to be. She will determine who she is by her actions and one thing is for sure, she will not be a victim.

'Yes!' She stands, slips her hand in her pocket, and pulls out the one thing that makes her feel a bit more secure, the one thing that gives her hope, the one thing she knows she cannot do without. Her passport.

Chapter 26

As he leaves the narrow bar, Loukas has a vague intention of finding Vlassis. Maybe if he talks to him some more, this feeling that something that he said has a bearing with his future will firm up, become more obvious. Something to do with Stella not giving them the bread order. No, something to do with if the old woman had the hotel's bread order, this would open up his future. But he is thinking with too much ouzo and brandy in his system and the clarity of his thoughts comes and goes with every step.

Saros is spilt into three parts. There is the new town, with new houses, new businesses, and sprawling international dealerships on the fringes of the municipality. Then there is the area that used to be thought as the poor area. Those who could not afford to live in the small, historic old town with its stone-built Venetian mansions. The poor area has recently become sought after. The people who live here form a community, and that alone is desirable these days. The families who live here are no longer poor.

But Loukas, as he staggers, is in the old town, which has lost so much of its sense of community as it is now made up of expensive holiday homes, hotels, and shops. The old town is pedestrianised—many of the streets here are too narrow for cars, and some are no more than cobbled lanes with steps at odd intervals, but the occasional motorbike flaunts the rules, weaving between the people. The area has become so desirable that there are very few shops offering life's staples. Somehow, the old town seems to have remained immune to the economic crisis gripping the rest of the country and the rents are too high to be afforded by those who peddle such mundane things as vegetables and fruits. But tucked away on one of the back streets, amongst fashionable boutiques and high-end jewellery shops, is one honest business that has continued to thrive. It is so successful it now owns the building, and there is no rent to pay for this institution—the Old Town Bakery.

The lights are out. The baker will be asleep. Loukas knows the bread from this shop is good but many times, he has heard it said that it is not as good as his. Here they also make biscuits and that he cannot compete with; he does not have the manpower. The Old Town Bakery also makes a good living on a Sunday when the people who come to their holiday homes for the weekends, as well as those fortunate enough to still live in these coveted dwellings, will bring a *tapsi* of meat and vegetables to be roasted in the big ovens. It is the traditional Greek way, from a time before electric ovens were common, and those with money and the stress of chasing after it hanker for these past times. It is also a good way to create a feeling of community now that every space has turned to profit-making in the old town. In the village, there is no such need: community is the one thing they have in abundance and the rural wives are still thrilled with their counter-top mini ovens. His bakery takes less and less to roast at the weekend and the old woman grumbles that their business is further affected by Stella and her chicken dinners.

Overall, The Old Town Bakery is far in advance of his humble village *fournos*. This is the business that supplies the bread to Stella's hotel.

He looks up at the three-storey stone-built building. The shutters are all newly painted, the ornamental brickwork edging the roof tiles all maintained and neatly pointed. He has no idea how many people are employed here on a daily basis, but he seriously doubts that they are really in need of Stella's hotel order. It will be a drop in the ocean for them. But for him, for the old man and old woman, it would increase their income substantially, if any of them were prepared to get out of bed an hour or two earlier to fulfil such an order.

There it is again. That feeling that the solution to his future is just in sight. It is probably just the ouzo giving him false hopes. More work is not the answer.

Where was he going? He was going to find someone. Who?

He passes the bakery's front door and catches the name of the owner on the hand-painted sign above the door. It is the same surname as Mitsos'. Everybody is related to everybody in these backwaters. That is the problem, interbreeding and nepotism. The whole of Greece is run on nepotism; no wonder the economy is in such a mess. If he thought he had a chance of a job, he would return to Athens. Any traces of hope for his future fade.

Few lights peep through closed shutters now and the narrow streets exclude the moon. Loukas plods on.

He seems to be going in circles.

Where was he heading?

'Hey Loukas.' Someone is shaking him. 'Loukas, come on friend, time to go home.'

Loukas blinks and sits up slowly. It is too much effort to have both eyes open so he opens just one. There is an unfinished glass of ouzo in front of him. He is in a bar in Saros. That much he does remember, but which one?

The pudgy barman puts his hand out to take the glass away and Loukas makes a move to stop him, but on second thought, he lets go. He has an almighty headache. Water would be a better choice.

'Come on *file*—friend,' the barman says again. The man in the framed poster on the wall above his head smiles down at him. Loukas does not remember returning here. The bottle of Metaxa in the photograph makes Loukas' stomach turn. He'd better leave quickly.

There are no taxis at the stand. Loukas looks at his watch. It is not surprising, considering the time. He will wait on the bench until one turns up. There is bound to be at least one on duty.

'Hey, mister.'

Is he doomed never to get any rest?

'Hey, do you know if there are taxis at this time of night?' The accent is Athenian. The speaker and his girl are smartly dressed. The man is holding the woman's shoes.

Loukas looks around to orientate himself, checks his watch, and then notices the orange glow on the horizon. He shrugs his shoulders in reply and looks blankly at the man. He cannot speak; it is too much effort. The man looks pointedly at the bench and Loukas swings his legs down off it so the couple can sit. Loukas staggers off towards the sea.

'Sea air,' he says to himself. 'That will restore me.'

With the sun just rising, the sea is on fire, the orange mingling with the silver and pale blue. Each step sobers him just a little and before he is halfway to the village, he is in a pleasant state where he is still just slightly drunk but his headache has almost gone. A bottle of water would be very welcome.

The path is of packed earth, trodden bare by many feet, and the cicadas are beginning to rasp their

273

love calls as the sun lights up the top of the oleander bushes by the way. The colour of the flowers is beautiful, uplifting even his black mood.

Someone is behind him. Why would anyone else use this path so early? The footfall is fast but regular. Are they trying to catch up with him? It is a good reason to stop, turn round, see who it is. Turning carefully so his head does not fall off proves to be a more difficult manoeuvre than just keeping one foot in front of the other.

'*Kalimera.*' The morning greeting is full of life and energy, and although Loukas does not immediately recognise his features, the running shorts, shoes, and vest tell him this can only be Fillipos, old Iason's son. 'Fillipos, I haven't seen you since you came back from your military service.' Loukas doesn't know Fillipos well—Fillipos began his national service soon after Loukas moved back to the village.

'Are you well, my friend?' The runner comes to a standstill, hands on hips, breathing heavily.

'Ach!' There is no other way Loukas can express his whole pointless existence succinctly.

'How come you are not making bread today?'

That is the last thing Loukas wants to talk about. He produced no bread yesterday, and, unless the old woman and old man are up, there will be no bread again today. That's all it will take, just a day or two, for the people of the village to find another source and the *fournos* will struggle. Then there will

274

be no reason for any of them to get up. He rolls his eyes as an answer.

'Such a great job; you are so lucky,' Fillipos enthuses. Loukas chuckles and frowns. The man has a strange sense of humour. 'No, I am serious,' Fillipos defends.

'Why on earth would you think such a job was good? It takes away your sleeping hours in the morning and kills any social life you could have in the evening.' Loukas starts to walk again but not with any speed, just strolling as the sun brings with it the heat as the day unfolds. Fillipos wipes his forehead on a sweatband around his wrist.

'Just that!' he replies. He pulls at his sweat-drenched t-shirt and flaps it, getting the air to circulate. 'I cannot understand anyone who would not want to be awake, alive right now!' He looks across the sparkling bay to the purple mountains beyond. 'Look at the colours, look at the light, feel the air, listen to the birds!'

Loukas struggles to do any of these things. He needs some water and a coffee. No, what he really needs is sleep. A really good night's, worry free, sleep.

'There are no colours, or light, or birds inside the bakery at this time.' Loukas shakes his head.

'But you can get up half an hour earlier, run under the stars, and still have the peace of this time to look forward to as you work.' There is no putting Fillipos off.

'I heard that you were not an evening person,' Loukas says.

'I never understood sitting in a smoke-filled bar, shouting to be heard. I can't see the fun in that. When we lose the light, we are designed to sleep. It is natural, is it not?' His voice is too full of enthusiasm.

Loukas tries not to chuckle.

'Don't you think?' Fillipos seems to need his agreement.

'Perhaps some people are for the morning and some are for the evening.'

'It seems there are not so many like me.' Fillipos chuckles good-naturedly. 'I am finding it hard to get a job that does not run into the evening.' Fillipos' energy subsides with his words. 'Stella offered me the bar job, you know? I might have to take it if nothing else comes up.'

'I didn't know.' But Loukas is not surprised. 'It's a good job,' he encourages, but he follows these words with a sigh.

Chapter 27

Sitting under the fairy-light-covered tree, Stella watches Mitsos sitting across in the *kafeneio,* ignoring her.

She shouldn't have snapped at him. But he is just going on and on about the legality of the hotel as if she can do something about it. Was it not enough that she has just come back from Saros town hall this morning? And Sarah! She never imagined Sarah would not support her. Well, that's not strictly fair, it is not as if Sarah is not supporting her, but surely she could manage a few more hours each day at reception. Everyone is expecting her to do everything by herself and the longer the hotel is open, more and more is being piled on her plate.

Kyria Poppy has started to make lace, and so she will have to find a bigger cabinet to display this in the lobby along with the carved olive wood bowls. She has had posters printed to tell customers that the garage in the village has a car that can be hired by the day, although maybe they should have bought something a little newer. But never mind, she will still support them. She will support anything that is positive for the village. The conversion of one of the storage cupboards into a beauty salon is going well and that will be opened next week by a girl from the village who does everybody's nails. Now the barber's daughter has asked if there is room for a hairdressing salon in the hotel somewhere. If only there was some support offered in return!

How can she be on reception half the day, man the beach bar at night, do the administration, manage the staff, organise the deliveries, *and* try to fight the planning department to stop them closing her if she does not get her paperwork sorted out? It seems the whole village is benefiting and taking all they can from the hotel but not stopping to offer help.

She slams her frappe glass down on the table with her eyes fixed on Mitsos, who looks so relaxed. He knows that in half an hour, the eatery will start filling with farmers and then she will be stuck and there will be no one on reception at the hotel when Sarah goes off to take out her goats.

'*Panayia!*' Stella utters a silent prayer to the mother of her god, crosses herself, and kisses the crucifix around her neck. Mitsos sits with his legs outstretched as Theo serves him coffee in a small cup and yes, that's an ouzo glass alongside it! Ouzo, during the day! The luxury! Well, two can play at that game.

Stella goes inside and round the back of the grill for a glass. There is washing up piled in the sink. If she wants an ouzo, she will have to wash a glass. She slings on an apron.

Half an hour later, the washing up is done. Several split chickens are on the grill cooking, and there is pile of sausages sizzling. Now she pours a good measure of ouzo and returns outside to stand beside the fairy light tree. Mitsos has not moved, still lazing in the *kafeneio* at the top of the square. She raises her glass to him, but he's not looking so she sneers and drinks.

The reception at the hotel will now be unmanned. He knows exactly what he is doing to walk out at such a time. So what if she is being unreasonable; who wouldn't be in her position?

'*Yeia sou* Stella.' Iason pulls up on his moped, takes a handkerchief from his pocket, and wipes his bald head.

'Your son going to take the bar job?' Stella snaps with no introduction.

'*Kalimera* to you too.' Iason smiles and banters.

Stella cannot return with anything jovial. With a last withering look at Mitsos, she pivots on her heel and goes inside. She will serve Iason and then go to the hotel. If other hungry farmers come, it's too bad today.

Loukas washes his face in the sea, lying face down on the village jetty. How can Fillipos choose to get up and run in such weather! After their talk this morning, he watched him run ahead and disappear into the village whilst he was still a good fifteen minutes' walk away.

He stands and shakes his head, the water spinning off him. He needs a shave but he cannot face going to the bakery. Mostly he needs to sleep but again, he does not want to even see the old woman. The only alternative is to wake himself up with coffee. Even that idea holds no motivation. Wake himself up for what?

He can see the hotel from here, a little way along the beach, with its colourful umbrellas and the outline of his beach bar.

'But it is not your beach bar, is it?' he mutters to himself. Pictures of Ellie swim through his mind. Ellie in her little dress. Ellie lying in the grass. Ellie under the plane tree drinking coffee in Saros. Ellie crying.

'Ellie.' He says her name out loud to tempt her image out of his head, but instead she sinks into his chest. He does not want her there; he will not give her that power. What she did was cold and cruel and unforgivable. There is part of him that is glad he will never see her again, but another part that would like to meet her to somehow make her suffer as he has done. He is glad he didn't see her to say goodbye; he wouldn't have been able to control himself, the words he would have spat! It would have taken more than a priest's blessing to forgive him!

'*Poutana*.' He mutters the disparagement very quietly, his heart not totally behind his words. Lying on the jetty, he allows his thoughts to drift, he knows not for how long, in and out of dreams and nightmares. Ellie walking up the aisle in the village

281

church to marry his old maths teacher, Loukas the ring bearer, walking behind them holding their marriage crowns. Making bread and talking to the old woman to slowly realise that he is now the old man with no future. But the sun is too bright to allow real sleep, nothing that refreshes him, and soon he gives up hoping for oblivion. Coffee, he needs coffee.

Instinctively, he returns to the track that leads directly to the village but once there, he hesitates before continuing on his way. If he wants caffeine, then it is the *kafeneio* he must head for. But how many of the men there will be complaining about their wives because they in turn are complaining about there being no bread? How many will complain directly because they have no bread with their meals?

'One word from anyone,' Loukas threatens the world as he walks.

The square is dozing in the sun. The village is unchanged. Loukas is surprised to see the bakery doors open, but there is no bread on the shelves. He knows it would not have all sold by now unless the old man got up late and only made a small batch. The positive side is that maybe no one will complain in the *kafeneio*.

The three steps into the café, even though they are concrete, are worn and dip in the middle. A testimony of a thousand footfalls, all male. That is as it has always been. A sanctuary.

There are several groups of men around different tables. A pair near the window are engaged in an energetic game of tavli and, to Loukas' surprise, there is Mitsos sitting on his own at a table in the corner at the end of the serving counter. That is where he would have chosen to sit. It is obscured by the flue pipe of the pot-bellied stove that heats the place in winter. The table is tucked away and privacy is implied. The men who frequent the *kafeneio* understand this and leave you alone if you sit there.

With reluctance, he pulls a chair from the table next to Mitsos'. The scowl on his face will tell people to let him alone.

Theo brings coffee and slowly the caffeine takes its effect, dissolving the mist of Loukas' hangover, but it does little to improve his mood.

A while later, Mitsos beckons Theo, who comes out from behind his counter and sidles past Loukas. Muttered words are exchanged and Theo bounces away and returns after a few minutes with two coffees. He serves one to Mitsos, but places the second one on Loukas' table, beside the coffee he has already drunk. With a twist of his hand, no words necessary, Loukas asks the question. Theo nods his head towards Mitsos.

'I am thinking you are both in trouble with the women in your life.' Theo nods gravely. 'This is what a *kafeneio* is for, to sort things out without the women interfering,' he says with no hint of humour. The bounce in his step is absent as he retreats. There is some irony to this last comment—Theo's own woman toys with him and has done so for years. And in his case, no *kafeneio* is likely to change the state of the relationship. 'Women from Athens are different,' he has remarked to Mitsos on more than one occasion. 'They do not respect the man's authority. But what can I do? I love her, even if she drives me crazy.'

The idea that Mitsos might be on bad terms with Stella does not sit well with Loukas. Mitsos is nothing but kindness and caring, and for all the initial anger he felt towards Stella with the Ellie episode has not remained in his heart, Stella is too dear to him for that. Without moving his chair, Loukas half-turns his body so he is side on to Mitsos, who is staring out of the window, down to the eatery.

'You not serving chicken?' Loukas asks.

'You not making bread?' Mitsos returns.

Loukas turns his chair slightly to face the older man.

'Stella?' Loukas asks quietly.

Mitsos turns to face him just a little.

'The old woman?' he asks in return and with a tiny movement of his finger, he points at the chair opposite him.

Loukas shifts across to Mitsos' table, taking his coffee with him. They sit in silence, each nodding their head every few seconds as if agreeing with something that neither of them are saying. After five minutes, Mitsos clears his throat.

'Sorry about the thing with Ellie,' Mitsos says but makes no attempt at eye contact, his gaze fixed on a point down the square.

'Women,' Loukas replies with the same blank look out at the world.

Mitsos grunts his agreement. They fall into silence again.

As they watch out into the sunshine, Fillipos, no longer in shorts, strides across the square toward the corner shop.

'He's changed,' Loukas reflects and points at him with a jut of his chin.

'Yes.'

'Loves mornings.' Loukas says this as if it is beyond his understanding.

'Needs a job.' Mitsos takes a sip of his coffee.

'He can have mine. Not that it is really a job. You're supposed to get paid for doing a job.' It is as close to humour as his mood will allow and neither of them laughs, but once he has said it, the idea plays on his mind. 'You know…' He pauses before finishing his sentence. 'If it was possible for him to take my job, then I could do the bar job and everyone is happy.'

Mitsos lets out a breathy snort through his nose.

'Until they close the hotel. Planning are really pressuring Stella.'

'Is it that serious?' Loukas asks. As Mitsos nods, there is that nagging feeling again. The one that came last night when he was talking with someone, who was it? Oh yes, what's-his-name, the old woman's nephew, Vlassis. He screws up his eyes to help his thoughts form.

'You alright?' Mitsos asks.

'Yes, just something, something, if only I was not so hung over, I can almost see.'

'See what? A fairy with a magic wind?' Mitsos says but he doesn't even smile. He is still watching the front of the eatery. Waiting to catch a glimpse of his beloved Stella, presumably.

'Yeah, right!' Loukas replies. He can think no more; if he is to talk, idle chit chat is easier. 'Tell me something, what is your relation with the Old Town Bakery?'

The night on the floor in the airport chapel has to be one of the most exciting nights she had ever spent. Part of the appeal was because it was a chapel, where sleeping would have been an unthinkable sin as far as Father was concerned. Through his eyes, it would show a lack of reverence, no respect. He would have gone ballistic if he had been there. But to her, it was the nicest thing the church has ever done for her: provide her with a warm, safe, carpeted place to sleep whilst she waited for her flight. The best thing about it was that no one else came in to disturb her the whole night.

She woke well in time and felt just slightly smug to see how many people had slept on the cold vinyl floor in the main waiting area. Most of these were young people too, although there was one woman with long grey hair and a multi-coloured jacket under her head and a colourful chunky-knit woollen blanket wrapped around her. Everyone else was young and cool, and Ellie felt excited to be one of them.

She finds am ATM and draws out more cash from her dwindling university fund.

'But this is going to be an education,' she reasons. Ellie cannot hold her joy inside; the words come out loud and although the man behind her pretends he did not hear, she can feel his eyes watching her as she walks away.

The flight is due to leave in an hour. She will be in Greece in four, and in the village in five or six hours.

'Oh Loukas.' Ellie feels she may burst.

Chapter 28

'So you are saying that The Old Town Bakery haven't got the hotel's bread order because they are your relatives?' Loukas says. They are on their third coffee and Theo has brought biscuits over. Really, they should find some lunch, but neither of them want to move. The *kafeneio* is a safe heaven, a retreat from the world. As long as they stay where they are, they are untouchable.

'No, no. It was just in with the package that Stella used to make the running of the hotel easier in the first few weeks. They deliver from Saros supermarket every other day, pick up the laundry, that kind of thing. The idea is that it is all smooth. But I think, if she can keep the hotel open, she wants to break it apart, you know, get the laundry done by someone who's a bit more reliable. They brought back the sheets but no towels last time and she wants to use the local butcher to support him, that sort of thing. But all that takes time.'

'Everything takes time.' Loukas thinks he sounds older than he feels when he says this. Time is what is weighing him down. The years ahead spent making bread, getting up early, living under the roof of his in-laws, denied his own life.

Fillipos marches back across the square again, returning the way he went.

Loukas' head jerks back as if a bee has stung him. He turns to Mitsos wide-eyed. His mouth is slightly open.

'What?' Mitsos says, looking across the square and thinking that whatever has startled Loukas must be out there.

'It's so obvious, it is staring us in the face. I cannot believe I have been so slow!' Loukas can feel new energies stirring.

'You have an idea?' Mitsos asks.

'Yes, yes, a solution!'

'Theo my friend,' Mitsos shouts across to Theo, standing behind the bar drying coffee cups. 'Two ouzos, and you'd better bring some olives. We need to sustain the boy; he has an idea.' Mitsos matches Loukas' turn of spirits. 'So, come on, tell all,' he encourages as Loukas formulates what he is about to say. Theo is quick with the olives and they both look up at him as he puts down the plate.

'You see, all you need is just a little time away from the women,' Theo chuckles, putting down two shot glasses and filling them with ouzo before returning to his counter.

Mitsos stabs an olive with a toothpick. 'Come on, I cannot be kept waiting!' he says.

'It will depend on you,' Loukas begins, and Mitsos looks intrigued. 'Do you think you could find a way to talk to your cousin in the old town bakery, explain to him that Stella needs to spilt up the package, that it is no reflection on the quality of his bread, that you want no argument, you know what I mean?' Loukas talks quickly. Mitsos is frowning, pondering but then starts to nod his head slowly in agreement.

'In that case, it is simple.' Loukas exhales his relief. 'If the village bakery got the hotel's bread order, the old woman could afford to pay a worker. But that person does not need to be me!'

And then he stops speaking abruptly and looks at Mitsos, eyebrows raised.

'Fillipos.' They say the name at the same time.

'Then I can take the bar job and everyone is happy!'

Theo's smile matches his own and his hand goes around his ouzo to lift the glass in the salute that Loukas is offering. But Mitsos' drink stays where it is and he shakes his head as if he is disappointed.

'What? Why not?' Loukas scowls.

'Well, for one thing your mother-in-law came to the eatery the other day and said some things she should not have said to Stella. I don't think there is any way Stella will give her the bread order now, not even if the old woman asked on bended knee!'

Loukas can feel his energy drain away as quickly as it was ignited. Just for a moment, he sensed his freedom, what it was like to choose his own destiny. Just for a moment, he felt like a man, not someone's boy.

'Also,' Mitsos continues, 'even if you did get Stella to agree to this, it doesn't alter the situation with the legalities at the planning department.' Mitsos slugs down his ouzo, but not with joy.

'Hang on,' says Loukas. 'I was talking to Vlassis last night. He really got under my skin and something that he was saying bothered me, like it meant something…'

'Vlassis?'

'You know, he works in the planning office. The nephew of the old woman.'

'Ah!' Mitsos exclaims as if it is he who has been stung now, and this time, Loukas is not keeping up. His hangover may be clearing but that doesn't mean he is thinking straight. 'I see what you are saying,' Mitsos says slowly. Which is more than Loukas does. He wonders if Theo will have any aspirins behind the bar, and rubs his temples. Mitsos continues, his slow speech suggesting he is thinking whilst he is talking. 'You get the old woman to talk to her nephew,' Mitsos says, 'to see if he can clear the way with planning. I can talk to my cousins to release Stella from the bread contract. Then the old woman and Stella can do an exchange. The planning in return for the bread order. Ha! With that order, the bakery will make enough to pay Fillipos to do your job and you can take the bar job, and the world is tranquil once more.' He exhales loudly and sinks into his chair, raising his ouzo glass, a satisfactory smile playing on his lips.

292

His excitement came through in his voice as he spoke and he looks up, surprised to see he has the attention of everyone in the room. Loukas is no longer rubbing his head. Instead, he has his own ouzo glass raised towards Mitsos and a big smile has brought out his dimples.

The other men in the café lift their glasses, following Loukas' lead, some shaking their heads, as they have no real idea of what is going on.

'*Yeia mas!*' Loukas shouts in return to Mitsos' speech, and all the old men in the bar back him.

'*Yeia mas!*'

'*Stin ygeia!*'

'*Sto kalo.*'

'*Yeia sou.*'

Each alters the toast according to their personalities. Although no one is really sure what it is all about, there is general chuckling and laughter and one by one, they return to their own conversations, their own affairs.

When Mitsos' glass is drained, he pats the air, implying Loukas should sit. Loukas is grinning, Mitsos is not.

'But what will it take to convince this, what was his name? In planning, your cousin. What will convince him to do this for the old woman?'

Loukas loses his smile; his dimple fades. His brow furrows, he shakes his head, shrugs.

'What do you know about him?' Mitsos says.

293

'Not much. He goes to a bar in Saros every night because he is lonely. Well, that's what the barman says.'

'Is he married?'

'I don't think so. He was looking at every girl that walked past the bar.'

'Really.' Mitsos' lips are tight and twisted to one side of his face; he is in deep thought. 'How high up is he in planning?'

'Oh, high enough to be able to push this through, I expect. There is only the deputy planning officer and the planning officer above him, and as far as I know, they spend their days in the *kafeneio*, leaving the work to him, this Vlassis.'

'Ah, so all we have to do is convince him that this is a good idea.'

'Why, what are you thinking, to bribe him? What if he tells the authorities? That will close the hotel for sure.'

'Oh no, nothing so obvious and direct. I am sure I will think of something when we talk to him. Come on.' He stands, puts some coins on the table, nods his thanks to Theo. Wandering over to a table where the local taxi driver is sitting, he whispers a word or two and with Loukas one step behind him, the three of them leave the *kafeneio*.

'Saros please, Yianni,' Mitsos tells the driver when they are all seated in the taxi. 'We need to go to the planning department.'

Chapter 29

The look on Stella's face as they approach the eatery would, under normal circumstances, be enough to make Mitsos think twice and perhaps retreat again to the security of the *kafeneio* until things have calmed down. But although he is by nature a timid man, he has also a boyish sense of excitement that spurs him on in this instance.

'And what is the purpose of you being here?' Stella spits at him as he steps into the eatery. Loukas wants to jump in, explain everything, for the two of them to be in love again but Mitsos holds up a hand and gives him a sideways glance.

'*Agapi mou,*' Mitsos begins. The air conditioning unit in the room with the tables and chairs creates a background hum.

'Don't you "*agapi mou*" me. One farmer after another has kept me here all afternoon whilst you have being knocking back your ouzos.' Stella throws a dirty plate onto the counter and the fork that's on it slides off and chimes on the floor, catching the sunlight as it does so. 'A girl from the hotel kitchens has taken it upon herself to answer the reception bell! What do you think that looks like to the public? Not exactly professional. All it takes is for a bad review or two, but oh no, drinking ouzo is more important to you!' Loukas has never seem her so angry, her shoulder-length hair more like a lion's mane, her kind eyes flashing with scorn. Although she is physically small, she is very intimidating.

'Ah, but I come with gifts of repentance.' Mitsos smiles. His weight shifts from one foot to the other as if he is excited.

'Too late. Get out, Mitsos. I don't need your humour. I need practical help. Just go,' Stella retorts, her movements not slowing, her anger not subsiding.

Loukas takes a step forward, ready to reassure her. Mitsos puts his hand up again, another sideways glance. Loukas becomes still.

'What would it take for you to forgive me?' Mitsos asks.

'If you don't go, I will throw you out myself.' Stella's eyes flash again.

'Stella, wait.' Loukas cannot control himself. Her gaze turns on him. It stops him in his tracks. Stella the pussycat, the sensitive calmer of all troubles, has her claws out, talons exposed. Loukas has no idea of what she is capable, and no desire to find out. His tongue sticks to the roof of his mouth.

'So, what is this gift?' Stella turns to give her attention to the pockets of Mitsos' jeans as if the gift is there.

'What would you like most in the world?' her husband asks her. Loukas wonders if Mitsos is pushing her too hard, teasing her, toying with her.

297

But the sparkle in his eyes says he is enjoying himself.

'Look, I am tired. I need to go to the hotel now you are back, so if you have something to say, just say it.' Stella relaxes her stance and leans against the upright fridge. The beer bottles inside rattle as she does so. She looks exhausted.

'You must tell me the answer, Stella. What do you want most in the world?'

Stella shuts her eyes as if to find some patience.

'World peace.' She sighs the words.

'No, seriously.' Mitsos does not seem to be able to stop himself.

'Okay. Seriously, all I want is for this planning to be sorted. That is my heaviest weight. Can you do that, Mitsos? Can you and your gang of one manage to perform that miracle?' She looks at Loukas as she says *your gang of one*.

'Done!' Mitsos says.

'Please don't tease. Mitsos.' She sounds as if all her fight has left her and she pulls her apron off and wipes her hands as if she is about to leave.

'It's true; it is done!' Loukas chips in.

Stella looks from Loukas to Mitsos.

Mitsos pulls, from his trouser waistband at the small of his back, an official-looking sheaf of papers. Stella uncurls the front page and reads the title and then thumbs through them. Her lips twitch. It turns into a smile. Her face lights up and she throws herself into Mitsos' arm and he kisses the top

298

of her head again and again. Their closeness, their joy, their love for one another feels so intimate, Loukas looks out into the sunshine, watches a dog sniffing at a stationary moped before it runs off down the street after a cat.

'Hang on.' Stella is looking at the back of the bundle of papers and she pulls herself away from Mitsos' embrace. 'This may be all correct and in place, but it hasn't been stamped.' She shows Mitsos and Loukas the dotted line with Vlassis' signature, but there also should be the official stamp. There is always an official stamp in Greece.

'Ah, well *agapi mou*, there is a small price that we must pay.' Mitsos' words drip like honey.

'How much?' Stella asks, her own voice hard and cold. Corruption in official places is, Loukas knows from their many talks together, one of Stella's pet hates.

'No money. But your ego may have to take a little hit,' Mitsos says softly.

'Why? What is wanted?' Stella says cautiously.

'The village bakery must have the bread order.' Mitsos waits for Stella to ask what this has to do with her planning, but she doesn't. She casts a look on Loukas. It is a look that Loukas would do anything to absolve himself from but before he has a chance to explain, Mitsos goes on. 'Once the village bakery have the order, and only after that is agreed, Loukas can tell the old man and old woman that he is leaving.' Stella's eyes widen at this. 'He can do this

299

because they will have the money to employ Fillipos to make the bread. Then you must offer Loukas for the bar job.'

The hardness of Stella's face creaks and his eyes light up as she smiles. 'Of course he can have the job in the bar!' She puts a hand on Loukas' arm as if to pull him into her, but then the implications of what Mitsos says seems to seep through and the smile fades and her mouth sets hard. 'You mean I am to give the old woman the bread order!' Stella's eyes are on fire again. She releases Loukas' arm.

'Is it too high price, *agapi mou*? If it is, I will say so. We will let them close us.' Mitsos puts his hand out to take the official document back. He clamps his fingers around the sheets and gives them a pull but Stella does not let go.

For a moment, there is a deadlock, nether pulling harder than the other until, with clenched teeth, Stella tugs the papers out of Mitsos' hands.

'Okay, but I am not asking her. Loukas, you can tell her.'

'Actually Stella, we have already tried that,' Mitsos says and Loukas can no longer look at Stella. Instead, he looks at the floor.

'Oh, I see, the old witch wants me to beg, eh?'

Mitsos sighs.

'If I beg, my prize is I get the hotel legal and Loukas working the beach bar,' she summarises. 'And she wants me begging her, to see me grovel at her mercy, lose my dignity because she would enjoy that!' Stella's words come out clipped.

300

Loukas can see that this might all go badly wrong. He has seen how petty the old woman is; maybe Stella is the same. He has never seen her in such a situation. Maybe all the villagers are the same. Oh God no, let her not be like that. He is so close to his freedom. He wills her with every ounce of his being.

'Please,' Loukas begins. But Mitsos' fingers twitch again for his silence.

The two men watch Stella's face, waiting. Her chest expands as she takes a breath, her lips tighten, the sinew in her neck taut until she explodes with, 'She does not know me!'

With no warning, arms swinging, head held high, she marches across the road and straight into the bakery. The bakery door slams behind her. Loukas can just hear the bell above the door tinkling on the inside and then all is quiet.

Loukas and Mitsos wait.

Mitsos fiddles with the latch on the fridge. It is an idle movement, not designed to fix the fault more than distract his attention, give him a reason not to make conversation with Loukas.

They continue to wait. The room seems to grow hotter. The last farmers leave, settling up with Mitsos, who seems glad of the distraction.

Then they wait again.

Time seems to slow to a standstill. Loukas watches the clock, the seconds ticking into minutes, the hand moving so slowly. He is waiting for the screeching sounds of the old woman's temper, the slamming of doors, the sound of things being thrown.

The phone rings. The noise not what they expect. They both look at it.

Mitsos clicks into work mode and answers it, tucking the phone under his chin, picking up a pen ready to write an order. He drops the pen and holds the receiver, looking at Loukas with wide eyes. He says 'oh' and then 'right' and puts the phone back in its cradle with a click.

'That was Vlassis,' Loukas says. 'He just got a call from the old woman to confirm that it is her wish that the planning goes through. He says if we are honourable about the other half of the deal, he will stamp the papers tonight.'

Loukas jumps on the spot, his fist clenched. The bakery doorbell tinkles across the road as Stella comes out, her head held high. Loukas has no idea what to expect now. Should he thank her? Should he stay silent? Should he take his lead from her?

'Right,' Stella says as if nothing has happened. 'The old woman has the bread order. Loukas, get yourself down to the beach bar.'

'Yes!' How does he hold in his excitement? He wants to hug her. His arms go out towards her but she does not respond. He feels awkward and then decides he will hug her whether she likes it or not and he throws his arms around her. Mitsos pats him. He cannot let her go, she is marvellous, astounding, wonderful. He pulls himself away far enough to kiss her on both cheeks.

'Alright, alright.' She releases herself from his grasp. 'Before you go to the hotel, you better go over there yourself and tell her you quit!' She indicates the bakery.

Loukas swallows and all his joy seems to drain from him. His arms fall to his sides limply. He had forgotten that he now needs to face the old woman himself.

He never thought it would feel strange pushing open the door to the bakery. He does not know what he expects to have changed but he feels so different, like the rest of the world should be different too. If Stella grovelled to the old woman, which is so hard to imagine, then what mood will the old woman be in? Smug? Righteous? Bitter? He really does not want to face her but this is the last step to his freedom.

They burnt the bread that morning. He can tell. The singed smell is still in the air. He wonders how many loaves. He hadn't noticed that when he was there just a couple of hours ago with Mitsos, before they talked to Stella.

The way Mitsos spoke to them about the bread order was all very civilized, and Loukas learnt a lot in that brief half-hour. Mitsos did not directly accuse the old woman of using her nephew to stall their planning application. Instead, he implied that she had more power then she could imagine, and did she know that? If she could do anything to get planning, help him out, the bread order would be hers. Not only that, but if she wanted to make biscuits, they would take small packs of them for the hospitality trays in the rooms, and would she be interested? He would be very grateful. For an old farmer, he was very eloquent in his speech, charming even. The old woman's gaze was fixed on Mitsos and Mitsos alone. Mitsos continued, and almost implied that the order was too much for his cousins in the old town bakery, that she would be doing a kindness not only to him but the town baker as well.

By the time Mitsos had finished, Loukas almost believed that without the old woman's agreement, the hotel and all the knock-on jobs for the villagers would not happen and it was she and only she who could set the village on this steady footing offered by the hotel's existence. Her bent frame straightened until she was sitting upright with such importance. Mitsos seemed to sense when to stop talking and the three men—Mitsos, Loukas and the old man—waited for her response.

She began to speak and Loukas felt his heart drop to his boots.

It would be so hard, she said. The extra demand on her would be so draining, she said, she was not sure she could do it. Did Mitsos not realise how old she was? Loukas was on the point of saying something but under the table, Mitsos' hand slid to his knee and squeezed it briefly, ensuring his silence.

'But if it is for the good for the village,' the old woman went on, 'then who am I to stand in the way of making so many people happy? If my bread assures work for the villagers and an increase in tourism for the area, then I will push my own feelings to one side and take on this burden. On one condition.'

It was then that the old woman said she would only agree to the proposal if Stella herself would come and ask. She wanted the village to know, all the village to know, that Stella had come to ask! Then maybe there was something she could do to make the paperwork go through.

Loukas wanted to spit on her, but Mitsos took her hand, raised it to his lips, and told her she was nothing short of a saint as he lightly kissed her withered fingers.

Now, through in the bakery, the old woman is sweeping the floor and the old man is cleaning the mixing machine. His mixing machine, that he designed and helped to construct.

The old women sees him first. She straightens her back and leans on the broom. The old man, sensing her stillness, looks up and follows her gaze. The sunlight filters through the shuttered window and picks up all the flour particles that have been driven into the air by the broom. The old woman has her faded pink flowered housecoat on and the old man's brown trousers are covered with flour.

Loukas has no idea what to say, how to start. He thought he would just tell them. State that he was leaving, offer Fillipos as a replacement but now he is here, it is not so easy. He would like to know what

Stella said, how she handled what she had to say. It must have been even harder for her.

'Stella was here,' he opens.

'Yes,' the old man answers, his eyes darting to his wife and back to Loukas.

'Did she ask?'

The old man looks to his wife, his gaze steady.

'She said she would be delighted if I would take the bread order. She said that it was only not offered to me at the beginning because of some package deal she had taken. If that had caused me any concern, she wanted me to know that she had many reasons why she would rather I took the order. But I do not think she has any idea of how much this will put us out.'

'But the bakery income will more than double!' Loukas tries to keep his voice steady.

'She is a good woman,' the old man says quietly. The old woman gives him a hard look.

'As gypsies go.' There is no hint of softness in her voice.

Loukas holds his tongue. It seems Stella just told the truth. She would in fact be delighted if the old woman had the bread order, although perhaps not for the reasons the old woman assumed. And telling them about the package deal was honest, too.

Honesty. Loukas internalises. Stella kept her dignity and got what she wanted with honesty. That was what Ellie didn't have. *Honesty wins, Ellie.* He tries to project the words from inside his head across the world to wherever she is.

'So, we will need to get up earlier,' the old woman states, bringing him back to the moment. 'We have a big order now. Someone will have to get out of bed at least an hour earlier, if not two.' Her broom begins to flick at the floor. 'That is something Stella and Mitsos did not think of when they came begging for me to do this thing.' She is almost talking to herself.

'Ah.' Loukas interrupts her. The old man, who has resumed cleaning the mixer, now stops to give Loukas his attention. The old woman narrows her eyes at him. 'Well, actually, I have a solution for the getting up early bit.' The woman's eyes narrow even more.

'Some people like getting up early, and some don't,' Loukas begins, trying to emulate the way he imagines Mitsos would handle the situation.

'We all know that.' The way the woman says it implies that his not liking early mornings is the problem. Loukas ignores her and continues.

'So, with the extra money, you can employ someone who is glad to be up so early, who enjoys that part of the day.'

'We cannot feed us three adults and afford to pay someone extra to work here. And where would we find such a person?' The old woman continues her sweeping as if the conversation is over. But the old man continues to wait, to listen.

'Let me go and employ Fillipos.' There, he has said it!

307

The flour in the air continues to hover. The heat from the oven creates a convection in the room and the dust takes a leisurely circle around all the corners.

They are all silent. Somewhere outside, a donkey bellows its raucous call, its heaving lungs losing power until the sound becomes a strange and strangling whimper.

'Fillipos, who is this Fillipos?' The broom slows to a halt again.

'Iason's son,' the old man clarifies. Loukas nods.

'He would take months to train,' the old woman grumbles.

'But he has such energy,' Loukas counters.

'I hear he's odd.'

'He is. He likes getting up early; he thinks working in a bakery would be the best job in the world; he has energy to spare, which he uses up going running at the moment; and, sin of all Greek sins, he doesn't drink or smoke.'

'Tell him to come,' the old woman says as she resumes her sweeping.

The old man nods at him, which Loukas takes as an agreement.

It is only as he is leaving the shop that he realises that no word was said about his future plans, no argument, no thanks, no well-wishing, no enquiry as to where he would go or what he would do. He was just ignored.

Loukas is surprised at how much this hurts.

309

Chapter 30

'Sex On the Beach, please.' The girl flutters her eyelashes at Loukas and her friend, in a matching orange bikini, giggles.

'Straight Sex or with raspberry liqueur?' Loukas asks with no hint of a smile. When they ordered their last round, he enjoyed flirting with these two Australian girls, but since then, he popped into the store cupboard and images of Ellie flooded his mind. Flooded his mind and pulled layers of thin healing off his heart. The raw wound hurts with every movement. He would like to be the sort of man who could flirt and play, maybe even have a succession of casual relationships, but in his depths, he knows that this is will never be him.

'Go on, crack a smile. Let's see those dimples,' the girl teases. There's a way he can grit his teeth to fake a smile and make his dimples appear. He learned to perfect this as a boy to divert scoldings over forgotten homework, to receive the largest bowls of milk puddings from his friend's mamas, and to be forgiven by his own mama when his boyish energy got him into trouble. He obliges the two girls in the same way and they giggle and pay for their drinks, waving away the change. Maybe with time, he could become that shallow mercenary type.

He watches their feet sink into the sand as they stroll back to their sun loungers.

Out to sea, the sun glints and reflects off every ripple and watery facet. The blue of the sky has deepened with the heat. Being here, looking at this view, this is his work now. There will be no pressure to go to bed, no pressure to be up early. He will see all of the day and enjoy the first stars of the night. The gritting of his teeth becomes a smile, but it is for himself.

'How are you doing?' It's Stella.

'Great!' Loukas replies, but the enthusiasm is missing.

'You know, there's something I've been wondering. What was the connection with the bread order to the hotel planning?'

'Vlassis!' Loukas says with delight, pleased with the part he has played.

'Vlassis?' Stella asks. 'The guy who is going to do the tours?'

'Yes. He is also the old woman's nephew. Works in town planning.'

'Ah.' Stella nods. 'That makes sense. So it was she who put the stop on it in the first place?'

'I didn't know, Stella. Not until last night.'

Stella is frowning and nodding. It is clear that this thought had not crossed her mind.

'I get it,' she says. 'So Vlassis gets a little payback.'

'Mitsos was clever.' Loukas pours Stella a lemonade and cuts a slice of fresh lemon, which he splits and hangs on the rim of the glass.

'When we went to see Vlassis, he was not pleased. First, the old lady is telling him to stop the papers going through, then he is asked to make it go ahead. He started complaining that he is not a pawn in other peoples' lives!'

Loukas' stomach was in a knot as they sat and talked to Vlassis. Mitsos suggested that they go to have coffee in the *kafeneio* where Vlassis' bosses spend so much of their time.

'It will make him feel as if it is in an official business meeting, make him feel important, like his bosses.' Mitsos and Loukas followed Vlassis from the town hall to the proposed place.

Mitsos took his time to explain the situation.

'So you see, if Stheno calls you to say the bread order is hers, you can agree to stamp the papers, yes?' Then he sat back, his job done. But Vlassis' face became hard.

'So I am to be played with. Pulled this way and that. My office is not a game. I have an important job. I do not see any respect being shown for who I am.' Vlassis had trouble getting his words out at first. Mitsos' face drained white and he took some time to wipe the coffee spills from the table with a paper napkin. Vlassis looked out across the road where a bus was pulling into Saros bus station and a gaggle of tall blond Scandinavian girls climbed off, pulling at rucksacks, opening maps.

'You know Vlassis, if the hotel was to stay open, those are the sort of tourists that would come. Streams and streams of them.' Mitsos sat up a little straighter, put down his paper napkin, and leaned in towards Vlassis.

Vlassis was blatant in his stares, the whites showing on three sides of his irises.

'What is that to me?' he replied, his teeth grinding as he finally turned away from the unfamiliar sight. 'They go around in groups. There is…'

'You are a genius, my friend!' Mitsos cut Vlassis short, slapping him on his back. 'It would take a guy like you to think of that!'

Vlassis frowned then and Loukas felt his own forehead crease but he lifted his brows and followed Mitsos' lead. Mitsos obviously had a plan, so he backed him with vigorous nodding.

'And you are the man to do it, Vlassis!' Mitsos laughed. 'Although you could hire someone else to take them if you didn't feel up to it, but yes, you are right, Vlassis. They would happily pay for a local to show them to the best bars, suggest to them, and guide them, to the best tavernas. Why, you would probably be able to agree a cut of the bill if you take a group or eight or more to any one place. I wish I had thought of it myself!'

By this time, Loukas had caught on. 'And the best bit is you could do it all after work, keep your town hall job and do this on the side,' he whispered as if it was a secret. Finally, Vlassis began to get the picture. 'They could sign up at the hotel, start from there. Stella could arrange it all and leave the rest to you! It's perfect, but of course, only as long as the hotel stays open...'

Vlassis looked back at the blond tourists, trying to hide the grin that was now splitting his face.

'He tried to act cool, you know, pretend he was doing us a favour, but we could see we'd got him,' Loukas laughs.

'Ah, that sounds like Mitsos. We have six signed up for tomorrow night already. I think it's going to be very popular.' She pauses and her voice takes on a more intimate tone. 'You know, Mitsos wasn't always like that. He used to be shy and unsure, a bit like you.' As she speaks, she looks past Loukas to some internal picture of her husband.

'But when we meet the right person, we change I think, eh Loukas?' Now she looks at him, her eyes slightly closed against the sun. 'Is your world complete, Loukas? Are you the happiest barman ever?' Stella stabs at an olive in a dish with a toothpick.

'Yes,' he replies.

'Nothing missing then?' Stella stops the olive halfway to her mouth. She looks at his face.

'That's unkind, Stella.' Loukas frowns. It is not like Stella to be cruel. He watches her eat the olive.

'What if she came back, Loukas? What would you do?'

'Nothing. Nothing will have changed. She is still married, she has still been dishonest with me, so nothing. I mistook who she was and I have learnt. I would run from someone like that now.' Loukas is emphatic.

'So if she suddenly appeared in front of you now, you would not speak to her? You would walk away?' Stella asks.

'Nothing has changed. She lied to me.'

315

'Well, she didn't so much lie as not tell you the whole truth.'

'It's the same thing.'

'What if I were to tell you her marriage was over?' Stella says this quietly.

'You have spoken to her? She has called?' Loukas retorts.

'No…' Stella begins.

'You know something?' Loukas balls the tea towel and throws it into the small sink. He misses and it falls to the floor.

'Well, it is not for me to say, really,' Stella says coyly.

Loukas' knuckles have gone white with the pressure of his fists so tightly closed.

'Stella?' He tries to sound calm, tries not to shout.

'Pass me the phone. I just need to call reception.' She holds her hand out in anticipation.

Loukas passes her the phone, she dials through, says the word 'yes' in English and presses the off button.

'Stella?' Loukas repeats. 'What is going on?' Stella looks in his eyes and holds his gaze to speak very intently;

'You know, I think that if a marriage is not from the heart, then it's worth less than the paper it's written on. Some things you just know are right and some things are not. Like our new part-time receptionist. I just knew she was right the moment I saw her.' Stella breaks their intense stare to turn away and watch a figure coming across the lawn.

Loukas puts his hand up to shield his eyes from the sun's glare. Whoever it is looks familiar. Her outline, the way she moves…

'Ellie!' He trips over a crate of beer in his rush to be released from the enclosure of the bar. Still stumbling, he runs.

'Ellie!' he repeats. They collide with force, his arms around her, soaking her in, drinking her up. He wants his chest to split open and absorb her; he cannot hold her tight enough. He needs to smell her hair, touch her skin, feel the beat of her heart.

'Loukas,' she mutters. She has tears in her eyes, her beautiful, soft eyes, her perfect nose, her exquisite lips. His mouth cannot wait, he wants to express his passion, to show his love, take her on the spot.

'Ellie,' he repeats, forcing himself to slow down, be aware of where he is.

'I am divorcing him,' Ellie whispers, but he puts his fingers to her lips. She does not have to explain. She is here and that is enough.

317

'You are mine,' he breathes. Out of the corner of his eye, he can see Stella has gone behind the bar and is putting on an apron, taking his place.

'Ellie,' he says again, looking deep into her eyes. He needs to be alone with her, out of sight of people. They need to find each other again, remind each other of who they are. It will not take long. He recognises her without words, but they need to walk, fall in step with each other, find each other's rhythms. With his arm around her, he steers her to the coastal path that leads to the village, towards the privacy of an olive grove with a small mud-brick cottage hidden in its depths. There is a For Rent sign pinned to the door.

He hopes she will like it.

If you enjoyed The Reluctant Baker please share it with a friend, and check out the other books in the Greek Village Collection!

I'm always delighted to receive email from readers, and I welcome new friends on Facebook.

https://www.facebook.com/authorsaraalexi
saraalexi@me.com

Happy reading,

Sara Alexi

14900080R00190

Printed in Great Britain
by Amazon.co.uk, Ltd.,
Marston Gate.